Mercier Press is the oldest independent Irish publishing house and has published books in the fields of history, literature, folklore, music, art, humour, drama, politics, current affairs, law and religion. It was founded in 1944 by John and Mary Feehan.

In the building up of a country few needs are as great as that of a publishing house which would make the people proud of their past, and proud of themselves as a people capable of inspiring and supporting a world of books which was their very own. Mercier Press has tried to be that publishing house. On the occasion of our fiftieth anniversary we thank the many writers and readers who have supported us and contributed to our success.

We face our second half-century with confidence.

INNOCENT BYSTANDERS
AND OTHER STORIES

JOHN B. KEANE

MERCIER PRESS

MERCIER PRESS
PO Box 5, 5 French Church Street, Cork and
24 Lower Abbey Street, Dublin 1

© John B. Keane 1994

ISBN 1 85635 084 3

A CIP is available for this book from the British Library.

10 9 8 7 6 5 4 3 2 1

TO SHEILA AND GEOFF
WITH LOVE

Printed in Ireland by Colour Books Ltd.

Contents

Innocent Bystanders

A woman accosted me in the backway recently. Her father, she informed me, was a peace-loving man who was never involved in an argument in his life. He was a daily communicant and as pious a layman as ever entered the sacred precincts of a church.

'He never raised his hand to one of us,' she said, 'and he adored my mother.' A tear appeared and there was a sniffle but she resumed control of herself and also resumed her gentle barrage. She told me that her father had once unwittingly been an innocent bystander for a very brief period of time. It was in the early 1960s. Some preachers or evangelists were holding forth outside the market place on the evening of the horse fair.

They spoke about God and the sinful ways of the world and, among other things, about the life of the world to come. The woman's father had stopped for a moment to listen. Although a devout Catholic he was a reasonably tolerant fellow and while he would have no objection if the interlopers were booted out of town he would not altogether approve, for instance, if they were hanged.

As he stood, his mind wandered and it was during this period that a tinker man, for no apparent reason, rushed from out of the recesses of the market place and struck him flush on the jaw. He did not fall. Rather did he stagger around the street and the roadway before being directed homewards by a passing Samaritan. A member of the civic guards pursued the tinker man but all to no avail. He might more profitably have pursued a snipe.

The guard concluded later that the tinker man for all his ferocity and hostility may have been basically a devout or even a militant Catholic. Who hasn't heard of the Church Militant! According to the guard the tinker man may well have mistaken our friend's unfortunate father for a member of the itinerant evangelists who were endeavouring to preach the Gospel.

'I mean,' said the garda, 'why else would he have struck him?'

It was the talk of the town that evening. I remember it well and as I endeavoured to console the woman who had accosted me I remember how my father reacted when he heard the news from a neighbour.

'All he was doing,' said the neighbour, 'was minding his own business and if a man can't mind his own business we had no business dying for freedom.'

Slowly, deliberately, my father took his pipe from his mouth. He frowned when the neighbour continued on about the injustice of the whole sorry business.

'Really,' said the neighbour in outrage, 'all the man was doing was standing there, just an innocent bystander.'

At this my father exploded although he was a civil man and quiet to boot, slow to anger and of a placatory nature.

'If,' said my father heatedly, 'he was an innocent bystander he must be prepared to accept the consequences and I say hats off to the tinker for showing such restraint for he might have kicked him as well.'

Such was my father's dislike of innocent bystanders that he would cheerfully have charged them with responsibility for all the woes of the world and for the outbreaks of all its wars.

As the woman chided me in the backway I managed to slip away. She stood there for a while chiding some neighbourhood curs at the injustice of it all.

Poor creature! She innocently believed that because a man is an innocent bystander he is guaranteed immunity from assault whereas the opposite is the case. He is a legitimate target for every passing blackguard and is simply inviting assault by his mere presence.

'Of all God's creatures,' said an angry relation of mine one time after he had been severely frustrated, 'the innocent bystander is surely the most provocative.'

'I would have thought,' my father suggested, 'that the adder or the viper would qualify before the innocent bystander.'

'No, no, no!' said the relative emphatically, 'they, after all, are only snakes and unless provoked themselves are relatively harmless whereas the innocent bystander sets out to provoke from the moment he bystands.'

He went on to cite an instance of this particular form of provocation. Apparently he was one day on his way to catch a bus which would take him to the city and to a very important appointment. As he hurried around a corner who should happen to be obstructing his way but an innocent bystander who stood with an umbrella in his hand looking at a concrete wall. A collision followed but our intrepid traveller continued on his way.

Shortly afterwards as he rounded a second corner who should chance to be standing at the other side deliberately barring the relative's way but another innocent bystander. There followed a second collision which floored both the bystander and the relative. Rather than retaliate the relative bravely rose to his feet and struggled manfully towards the bus stop.

By now, badly battered, his gait had slowed but he managed to remain upright. Then just as he entered the station who happened to bar his way for the third time but another innocent bystander who chanced to be needlessly studying the sky overhead. So slow was my relative's pace at this stage that the ensuing collision should have been inconsequential. Alas my unfortunate cousin was at the end of his tether and very nearly collapsed. He had just enough spark left in him to deliver a well-judged kick to the skywatcher's posterior. He would have kicked him a second time but instead settled for a straight left at which particular punch he had developed a proficiency over the years. Expecting some form of accolade from my father he sat himself down exhausted at the end of his narrative.

'You should be ashamed of yourself,' said my father. 'You permitted three vile criminals to go free when you might have reported their obnoxious and murderous behaviour to the authorities. You have granted them a licence to further provoke God-fearing people and you have shamed yourself and your family by not acting responsibly towards your fellow man. It is we who shall have to suffer from your lack of patriotism until the three innocent bystanders you encountered are safely incarcerated or under the clay.'

So saying my father rose, donned his hat and went out into the world. The relative and I were agreed that there was some substance to what he had said and were glad that we were not innocent bystanders intent on their provocative ways within the ambit of my father's peregrinations.

Pernounciations

Some men are born to be great, others to be failures. There is, however, the consolation that the failure has the same chance of being happy as the great man. Greatness is no guarantee of happiness. Of course, neither is failure. It must be said at once that some words, like people, are born to be great. Others, alas, are born to be failures.

Let me explain. You have words like beautiful and you have words like brilliant. They are much in use and, most important of all, they are pronounceable. Other words, for instance, like investigation and recognition to mention but a few, while easily pronounceable to some are unpronounceable to others.

A man arrived into the pub one day bearing a plastic bag which carried the remains of an ancient timber plough.

'I wants this westergasted,' he said, 'and someone said you'd be the man to do it.'

At the time I did not know what westergation meant. I stole into the kitchen and consulted my wife.

'That's easy,' she said. 'To westergate is to investigate. Some people call it westergate,' she continued, 'and cannot see what's the use in putting an 'in' before it.'

So that was it. He simply wanted me to investigate his wooden plough.

Recognition is another unfortunate word which has

suffered from many different and incorrect pernoun-
ciations, sorry pronunciations. The late Jack Faulkner,
the great travelling man, used to say that he had a
cousin in Clare who was a brilliant man, 'but,' said
Jack, 'he can't even pernounce his own name'.

I sympathised and Jack proceeded to inform me
that he knew hundreds who went to school and who
could not pernounce the simplest of words.

'When I was in the army,' said Jack, 'you had to
pernounce your words properly or you could be killed.
There was a drunken corporal coming home one night
and refused to halt when I ordered him. I was on sen-
try duty and I had a loaded gun.

'"Advance to be reckernised," I called.'

'"What do you think he called back?" Jack asked.'

'"I give up," I answered.'

'"Is that Faulkner?" he shouted.'

'"Tis me," said Jack.'

'"I'm so drunk," said the corporal, "that I don't even
reckernise myself."'

'"Tis a good job,' said Jack, "that one of us knows
who he is or you'd be a dead duck by now."'

There was another occasion in the bar when two
teachers were discussing a trigonometry paper which
their pupils had found extremely difficult. There was a
third man in the bar at the time who had considerable
difficulties with pronouncing long words. The third
man was drunk and aggressive. He persisted in interfering with the teachers.

'Do you know something about trigonometry?' asked one of the teachers.

'Triggernomerty is it!' he said disdainfully. 'Nomerty is a cowboy I'd say and don't every fool know what a trigger is.'

The teachers enjoyed the input but the man who inputted did not. He was one of those individuals who believes that when people laugh in his presence they are laughing at him. A row followed and one of the teachers who had a short fuse floored Triggernomerty, as we'll call him, far better than any sheriff ever could.

Mispronunciation can land a man in deep water. I had a man working for me once and he had a problem with words. I engaged him for a period of one month. His job was to whitewash the backyard and the exteriors of the outhouses, to clean out the eaves' shoots and to place pieces of plaster in holes previously occupied by plaster which had been evicted by those relentless intruders wind and rain. One afternoon he came to me and said that 'better than whitewash' would be needed for an outhouse door.

'Whitewash is all right,' he conceded, 'but paint it ain't.'

It transpired that there was a half tin of paint in the store, 'but,' said he, ''twill take porpentine to thin it out.'

Porpentine! Where had I heard the word before? What he meant was turpentine, but we both knew what was required and that was the important thing.

That night as I sat drinking a pint with a friend it all came back to me. Readers will recall that part of *Hamlet* where our hero is addressed by his father's ghost:

I am thy father's spirit,
Doom'd for a certain term to walk the night ...
But that I am forbid
To tell the secrets of my prison-house
I could a tale unfold whose lightest word
Would harrow up thy soul, freeze thy young blood,
Make thy two eyes, like stars, start from their spheres,
Thy knotted and combined locks to part ...
Like quills upon the fretful porpentine.

So we see gentle reader that if you were to put a porpentine into a half tin of paint instead of turpentine
there would be disastrous consequences. The moral is
that we should ponder well before we deliver verbal
broadsides which could provoke the same reaction as
shrapnel.

I remember well to have been loitering in the vicinity of an ice-cream stand at Ballybunion many years
ago. A small man, accompanied by a wife and five
children, placed an order for seven cartoons of ice-
cream.

'Cartoons!' the youngster behind the counter scoffed. 'Go up town to the cinema and you'll get all the
cartoons you want.'

The small man shot out a left fist. The youngster
fell. The small man moved with his party to the next
stand and was accommodated without comment. If the
small man had said carton instead of cartoon there
would have been no trouble. If the youngster had used
his imagination, he wouldn't have been floored.

The Makings of a Book

Once upon a time my wife disclosed that she was going to write a book called 'In the Round of a Day'.

In it would be detailed the fads and fancies, all the sayings and descriptions of the apparel worn by the customers who visited the bar from opening time to closing time. When the day came to an end she discovered that not a memorable human being had called.

It was just one of those days. I told her she should try another day but she never bothered. When I was left in charge of the bar for the better part of a day last week I decided to take up where she had left off. I did not start recording the sayings and antics of my visitors till half-past three in the afternoon but by the call of time many hours later I had the makings of a small book.

It was that kind of a day. The first arrival was a man made like a totem pole except that his face was more intimidating. He was as drunk as a brewery rat so I sent him on his way. He covered me with assorted curses before he left.

Then came a party of three people from Clare. They required ham sandwiches with their drinks so I invited the youngest of the party, a ten year old girl, into the kitchen and we made the sandwiches together in jig time. When the sandwiches were made I asked her if she could dance a step.

'I'll dance if you can didle,' she said. So I didled

while she danced. The oldest of the Clare men told of a time when every house in the Clare countryside never missed the Rosary.

'My mother,' he said, 'was very slow so what did my brother Mick do, God be good to him, but take a few beads out of each of the decades when she wasn't looking.'

Apparently the deceit worked for a while but when she found out she added the missing prayers, the appropriate number each night, until all were accounted for.

'The war was the best time,' another old man announced. 'It was all bicycles and if your bike hadn't a Brook's saddle there was nothing thought of you. They were the most valuable things around, worth their weight in gold almost, in silver surely.'

There was silence for a while. They downed the sandwiches and complimented the makers. Then a small, bald-headed man entered and he shook hands with the oldest of the Clare men. During the war they had been in the Local Defence Forces together. There was much rejoicing while they reminisced about the good old days when they scoured the countryside for Germans and their only weapons flash lamps.

At that time you'd have to be six weeks in the force before your time for free boots came round. One night their commander told them that they would have to devise a strategy for capturing Germans should there be an invasion.

'What about my boots?' a recruit asked. 'I'm seven weeks in the outfit now and no boots.'

'What size do you take?' the commander asked.

'Seven and a half,' came the answer.

'All I have is one pair of size eleven,' said the commander.

'They'll do,' said our man, 'boots is boots and I have plenty of socks at home to fill out my feet.'

I told them of the night in 1939 when my brother Eamon came cycling down Church Street dressed in my father's hat and overcoat. In one of his hands was a homemade megaphone into which he shouted every so often that the Germans had landed. He woke up the whole street and when he came home he slept the sleep of the just.

Other stories followed and dances and songs. Sure I could write a book about it if only I had the space.

Then a bowsie came in. He could not complete a sentence without using the four-letter word. Now, anybody in a moment of rage or desperation can use a four-letter word but the constant use of this colourless expression jars me to the hilt.

'Vary your diction,' said the Clare girl at which he expostulated all the more and let loose a veritable torrent of the words in question.

We decided to ignore him. After a while he went away. I heard later that he was thrown out of every pub in the town.

'During the war,' the oldest of the Clare men began his story, 'the army came out our way and pitched their tents in Mohan's field. They weren't long in finding a house where there was a widower and his four daughters. The widower had no objection but he didn't like the soldiers to stay too late. Once he was awakened from his slumbers at four o'clock in the morning and he warned the soldiers that he would cut the heads off 'em with an axe if it happened again. I declare to God didn't the same thing happen the following Wednesday night which is the day the soldiers got paid their thirteen and tuppence a week.

'They wakened him up again and this time it was half-past four. The four daughters and about ten soldiers were dancing and singing fit to burst.

'He put on his wellies over his long johns and made down for the kitchen with the axe in his hand. The minute the soldiers caught sight of him they bolted. He followed them to the door roaring after them like a madman and he swinging the axe no end.'

Here the Clareman paused to draw breath before going on. He swallowed from his glass of stout and carelessly collected some crumbs from the plate where the sandwiches had been.

'The man with the axe, apparently, followed the soldiers as far as the cross but don't ask me what cross it was.

'"Ye're nice militia,' he crowed after them. "Ye're the bucks what's supposed to fight the Germans and ye running from an oul man with a hatchet!"'

So the day wore on and by the end of it I had the makings of two books, not to mind one.

Whiners

'I'd love to resign,' I heard a man say lately, 'but I'm a member of nothing.' People are always at it, going on and on about giving up, cnawshawling and carping morning, noon and night, addling their families and their spouses with complaint after complaint.

When they're not going on about a daughter-in-law it's a brother-in-law and when it's neither it's a sister-in-law or a mother-in-law. Perhaps you gentle reader are obliged to listen to this ongoing session of complaining and whining yourself and perhaps you are growing tired of it. Perhaps you are saying to yourself 'I'm putting up with no more of this', or 'I'll pack a suitcase and I'll get the hell outa here', or 'why do I have to listen to this day in, day out!'

Let me issue the direst warning. Under no circumstances complain about your lot. Listen to what the whiners have to say for as sure as God made little apples if you don't they'll do something worse. For every whiner there has to be a listener so listen and enjoy it. However it might be best not to smile and whatever you do don't laugh. Laughter in this instance is provocative and whiners are bad enough without provoking them.

When I was a garsún I used to visit, on my mother's express instructions, an aged relative who lived not too far away. My younger sister used to come with me on such occasions. We would minister to the aged relative and run errands and wash spuds for her or scrape the carrots. We would clean the windows and brush the floors to the best of our ability and never once did we receive a single penny or a single word of thanks. At first we found her intolerable but then we began to enjoy her. We would hold back the mirth when she spoke about her bowels and castigate them severely for their lack of movement.

When she spoke about her gas we would often have to run out into the backyard lest we explode. She never caught us smiling or laughing as we did exactly as our mother told when the old woman upbraided and lambasted us. We offered it up. My mother never said where 'up' was but we presumed that it was up to heaven or to Our Lady or even to God. When we grew older a younger sister and a neighbour's daughter were sent in our place. We were all set for secondary school and my mother felt we had suffered our share although she never said so.

Those visits to that old woman were the best schooling we ever had. Then she took seriously ill and we went to see her. We were astonished to discover that she had stopped complaining even though she was on her death bed. How is it, we asked ourselves, that people complain when they have no cause to complain and remain silent when they have every right to complain!

Complaining, I am convinced, is an art form. A person who is unable to complain or whine or cnawshawl will do no good in this world. I remember a woman who fell off her bicycle after she was attacked, for no reason, by a terrier. She was unconscious for hours and when she woke she was informed that she had been examined from head to toe but the doctors could find nothing wrong.

'I'll live all right,' she said, 'but I'll do no good.' She was disgusted, of course, by the fact that she was left with nothing to complain about when she might have had a bonanza.

People who complain are secretly enjoying themselves and it is only fair that those who have to listen should also be allowed to enjoy themselves.

My sister and I knocked great satisfaction and enjoyment out of the old lady we used to visit. She was a great character. The only time I ever heard her give thanks to God was when she broke wind. Then she would make the sign of the cross and give thanks to Almighty God.

This would be followed by comments like 'better in than out', and 'I won't know myself for a while now'.

Belching also brought expressions of gratitude. She had a most colourful vocabulary. Sometimes when her innards rumbled she would say 'them are gases fighting each other'.

She died blissfully in her sleep without a chirp out of her. I'm certain that she gave out to Saint Peter if he kept her waiting. She had no patience and would wait for nothing here on earth. She was the greatest whiner I ever knew and I sorely miss her.

Long Sentences

Listening to the radio I was struck by the fact that politicians are masters of the long sentence. By the constant use of buts, ifs and ands to mention but a few overdone conjunctions they seem to go on *ad infinitum* even when frequently interrupted by other politicians and by the person conducting the debate.

When asked for an answer such as yes or no they accept the question as a licence to go on and on with the end result as inconclusive as ever. Good as our southern politicians are, however, in respect of marathon formulations they wouldn't hold a candle to their northern counterparts, but I will concede that they are catching on fast.

The idea is, of course, that the longer the sentence the fewer the interruptions since it is considered bad manners to break in at the middle of a sentence. Just as one believes that the northern politician is about to cease he unexpectedly comes out with: 'and if I may say so', or 'on a point of order', or 'but on the other side of the coin'. These short phrases are merely the links that assure longevity. I have listened while those waiting in the queue so to speak made bold bids to get in their tuppences worth but it's all to no avail once the speaker is in his stride. Fear of interruption is the motive and the content of the sentence does not seem to matter as much, in the final analysis, as the length.

You can have sentence after sentence after sentence with nothing being said but there is with the solitary, long sentence, always the possibility of a candidate for the *Guinness Book of Records*. I don't know what the longest sentence is at this precise time and I don't even know if sentence records have been recorded but I do know that it would take a very long sentence indeed to surpass those of our Irish politicians both north and south.

I once read of an obscure tribe of South Sea Islanders called the Manata who used to form group sentences which lasted for hours. There was no written speech form so you'll have to take my word for it just as I take the word of the explorer who first discovered the Manata. For instance a Manata warrior might arrive home in his gumja (coracle) one evening and enter the great hall of the village headquarters announcing: 'I have seen a pedigerous mackerel walking on top of the water.' Now, all the Manata knew that mackerel never walk but do they say the news is without foundation the way our Irish politicians would! Not at all. They know the guy is a pathological liar just as his father and mother were before him but they don't come right out with it. What happens is that the nearest Manata to him continues on in the same vein although, truth to tell, disparagingly.

'And I have seen a pedigerous corset,' he says, 'with nothing inside in it.'

'And,' says the next man, 'I have seen a pedigerous coconut and I in my bed all day which prompts me to suggest that God only knows what I might have seen if I had been out and about.'

'And I,' the head or Chief Paloodrum goes on, 'saw a man with no behind but having two navels and this despite the fact that I was feeding the hens at the time since my wife has sprained her ankle and it prompts me to suggest that had I not been feeding the hens and free to look around properly I surely would have seen sights that exceeded anything ever seen before.'

'And I should perhaps say,' said the Manata who brought home the news of the pedigerous mackerel, 'that perhaps after all it was a legless mackerel I saw and what I took to be legs were merely splashes of water.'

So we see gentle reader that it is not by contradicting liars that we make them tell the truth but rather by exaggerating in the same vein, thus forcing them to recant.

Would that our politicians might behave thus! For instance when a member of the opposition promises his listeners more money when his party gets into power the leader of the ruling party might say: 'and I'll provide free leather bags to hold this money if the deputy doesn't think me too forward.'

Obstructors

Recently I spoke to the proprietor of a funeral parlour in the city of Dublin. He had read some pieces of mine about the ups and downs of the undertaking business and he told me that he was impressed. That is why he left the party with whom he was drinking and made his way from one end of the bar to the other in order to compliment me.

I asked him a number of questions about undertaking. Firstly I asked him why they were called undertakers in this country. He smiled.

'I suppose,' said he, 'it's because we takes 'em under.'

The bane of his life, he informed me, were queue-breakers who line up to sympathise with the relatives and then break ranks when the queue doesn't move fast enough for them. I informed him that we had transgressors of the same nature down the country except that they did not even line up. He could scarcely credit it when I told him they just by-passed the queue as if it didn't exist. He was astonished but even more astonished when I revealed to him that there were some mourners who formed queues of their own when faced with joining a long queue which had been there already.

'They should be prosecuted,' he said angrily. 'A few months in jail wouldn't be long curing gurriers the like o' them.'

We both believe, after lengthy discussion, that most of these funeral queue-breakers belong on the stage. They show tremendous acting ability as they approach the funeral parlour. They give the impression that they do not know what a queue is. The expressions on their faces would have their victims believe that they have never seen a queue before. I have seen them myself as they paused with wry expressions on surprised faces. Their lips seem about to frame the question: 'what manner of contraption is this? Let us ignore it for God's sake and pass on. Let us not encourage these foibles in those inconsiderate eccentrics who would have us do as they do and misbehave by joining this long obstruction!

'Let us not suffer these fools gladly but rather let us go on our own way no matter how inconvenient it may be for those guilt-ridden louts who would expect us to behave like them!'

Let us now look at the inside scene where the next-of-kin are gathered. The deceased naturally holds pride of place where it lies in the coffin at which everybody pauses for a moment or two before moving on. Some pause to have a good gander at the clothes and the coffin and to value the latter so that they may carry the news far and wide that the coffin was an inferior one or an expensive one.

Others pause to say a prayer or two and still more pause to see whether the corpse is handsome or emaciated. They like to be informed of such aspects of the obsequies.

About one in every three pauses out of reverence

and respect for the dead and particularly for this individual cadaver. You see, the fact of the matter is that
most people enjoy funerals and the sense of loss is
secondary. I personally don't enjoy funerals because of
the behaviour of certain mourners, the most obstruc-
tive of all being those who stop and start conversations
with the next of kin while a huge pile-up of would-be
mourners delays the proceedings no end so that
funerals often run late causing great distress to
mothers of families and others who have vital com-
mitments.

These obstructors are female for the most part and
they show no consideration for those in their wake.
They bend over the seated mourner with large posteriors extended as they pose questions about living members of the family of the deceased. So extended is the
posterior that it is impossible to pass. The obstructor,
male or female, heeds not the whispered pleas coming
from behind. Instead the posterior is seen to flicker
indignantly at the slightest touch.

Outside the funeral parlour the queue grows longer
and longer and still the indoor obstructor does not
budge an inch. Finally the next-of-kin to whom she is
addressing herself closes her eyes and pretends to fall
asleep. Reluctantly the obstructor moves on seeking
another source of information. These people make or-
deals out of funerals and turn many genuine mourners
away. The cure is to by-pass them and to ignore the
member of the next-of-kin who suffers them for she
must shoulder a fair share of the blame. It could, in
fact, be said that she could also be prosecuted for aid-

ing and abetting. After all she encourages the obstructor to loiter in the first place by not reminding her of her obligation to move on and make way for other mourners.

Worst of all is when a pair of obstructors, upon recognising a familiar face among the ranks of the next-of-kin, greet her as thirsty Arabs greet an unexpected oasis. They enquire about all manner of things from the quality of the year's potatoes to the condition of the silage. While it is sometimes possible to slip past one it is physically impossible to slip past two so that the queue lengthens. In many respects it resembles a traffic jam except that there is no recourse to members of the Garda Síochána. Funeral parlours are places of peace and repose and forcibly removing obstructors, however provocative, would be a distinct let-down to the next-of-kin.

The ideal answer is, of course, an MC. There are MC's at weddings and why shouldn't they be at funerals. I foresee a drastic drop in the number of funeral-goers unless things change in the very near future. Young people these days have neither the patience nor the energy to survive marathon funerals.

This is not my first time holding forth about time-wasting inside and outside funeral parlours. We must not lay the blame on the proprietors. You cannot walk up to a person at a funeral and tell them to move on. I have never met a funeral-parlour proprietor who was offensive.

They have to remember, I daresay, that everybody dies sooner or later and a body who has been pushed about so to speak at a funeral parlour will not be likely to nominate the proprietor of the parlour in question to take charge of the removal of his or her remains.

On the other hand the proprietor who has a friendly smile for all whether they are obstructors or not will be rewarded by the ultimate favour at the end of the day.

Tuning Up

Many years ago my wife and I went to the local cinema to see the film *From Here to Eternity*. We went at my insistence since I had read the book and was intrigued by it. The reason my wife was reluctant to go was that she was expecting visitors. So what! the gentle reader will interpose. So what! Visitors come and go but life must go on. Cinemas must be visited, meals prepared, groceries purchased and all the other mundane business of living accomplished before day's end.

Easily said my friends. These, let me say at once, were visitors with a difference. Let me explain. One of the visitors was a local fiddle player and while he was in hospital in Tralee convalescing after an operation he met two other fiddlers from different parts of the county, one from mid-Kerry and the other from Castleisland. They vowed, before they left the hospital, that they would meet again.

Of all the brotherhoods known to man the brotherhood of hospital mates is the most enduring. It is as enduring as the sea and as vibrant as the stars. Old-boy networks pale by comparison and reunions between one-time patients go on till the members expire.

There is a camaraderie which is only to be found among the survivors of shipwrecks who have faced thirst and starvation on inhospitable beaches and trackless interiors. I have long been convinced that true friendships are born out of hardship and that friendships otherwise established are as fickle and changing as the shapes of the clouds that move over our heads.

We were somewhat annoyed that the visitors had selected a night for which we had planned an outing in advance. They arrived at twenty-five minutes to eight. They were three in number and each bore a fiddle as well as a bow. None had fiddle cases. This does not mean that they were rough and ready musicians. Rather were they country musicians who had long since dispensed with unnecessary baggage. They came by hired car and would return to their abodes by hired car at the very witching hour of night.

We greeted them warmly and they, for their part, expressed delight at the fervent manner in which they were greeted.

'We are humble musicians,' said their spokesman, 'and ye are high-up townies and don't think we don't appreciate what ye are doing for us.' I knew at once that I was in the presence of rogues, likable rogues. What else could I do but stand them a round of drinks! They gladly accepted saying that there was no need or no justification for such unprecedented generosity. Just then the local fiddlers arrived led by the man who had spent time in hospital with the spokesman for the visitors. They were also invited to have a drink although not by me. I'm sure they felt it was enough that I should pay for it.

After the drink was filled and distributed we pointed out to them that we would be going to the cinema but that we would be back in a few short hours. Meanwhile they were to make themselves at home and make the rafters ring as it were. As we left they were embracing each other like long lost brothers.

Time passed and we returned. From the back kitchen, or lounge as it is called now, came the sounds of fiddle music. We called the girl in charge during our absence to find out how things went during the night and she replied that a single tune had not emerged from the interior. There had been scraping and squealing alright but no melody.

With mixed feelings I opened the kitchen door. I could barely discern the fiddlers through a dense haze. The floor was covered with what seemed to be snow. The fiddlers were in the throes of a most unholy cacophony. An explanation was quickly forthcoming from our deputy. The snow on the floor was not snow at all. It was the residue of the resin which the fiddlers had been applying to their strings all night as they tuned up. So committed were they to the meaning of melody that they had spent two and a half hours tuning up without producing a single tune. Their faces radiated happiness and if they had a few pints taken itself you would not find a more harmonious company if you were to search from Mizen Head to Malin Head.

They were to spend another hour and a half in the fiddle room which was the elegant name our visitors had bestowed on our humble back kitchen. One unkind commentator insisted that they had wasted so much time drinking porter and whiskey that there was no time left for music. Another claimed that they were so incapacitated by booze that they were quite incapable of rendering a tune.

What mattered to my wife and I was the happiness of our visitors and to a lesser degree the happiness of our local fiddlers who were responsible for the session in the first place. All one had to do was to sit in their midst and behold rather than listen. Talk about rapture on the faces of all. Talk about goodwill and kind feelings for each other. They tuned away blissfully with little notion of starting a tune. It was a jaundiced critic pointed out to an equally jaundiced companion, a lot easier to tune up than to play a tune.

This criticism was totally unfounded. I submit that any fool can play a tune on a fiddle but only a real musician can tune up. Their revelry, seemingly barbaric and disorganised to the ignorant listener was part of the real rapture of fiddle music.

In many ways they had the same lofty pursuit as Jason and his followers who went in search of the Golden Fleece. At another, more realistic level they reminded me of the search for the Lost Chord. They knew that they would never find it but they would go on trying nevertheless. The search would never end. Sooner or later somebody would embark on a legitimate tune and the holy search for perfection would end. The fiddlers knew this and so it was that the gallant brotherhood of countrymen and townies united in our fiddle room for one of the most exhaustive searches ever made for the realisation of their musical dreams. What an honour to have hosted such a gathering!

Not before or since have I heard anything quite like

it. They have gone now, all of those incomparable fiddle men and we shall not hear their likes again.

False Account

There are tale carriers whose slightest utterances cannot be believed. There is no community without one and indeed there have been standard names for them down the years such as Dick the Liar and Tom the Liar and so forth and so on.

Then there is the tale carrier whose tales have become so distorted in transit that nothing remains in the end but a parody of the original.

Then there are what I call natural tale-carriers. Everything you hear from the natural tale-carrier should be divided by at least two or even three. The net result will provide you with a semblance of the truth.

Only last Sunday week I was at a football game in Ballybunion. There was a good crowd and the game which was contested provided high class entertainment.

That night in these here licensed premises a man held forth about the same game until I was forced to draw the conclusion that we were at two different games. According to him the fare was substandard and there was hardly anyone present. I contradicted him and informed him that where I sat in the sideline there seemed to be quite a good crowd.

'Well,' said he, 'I was in the stand and there wasn't enough of us there to put a ring on a sow.'

Instead of dividing by two or three in this instance

one should multiply by a hundred. The problem with this tale-carrier was that he didn't care for Bally-bunion and why should he for wasn't he the victim of several bad decisions there during the Pavilion dances for which the resort was once famous.

On one particular night he devoted all his attention to one girl. She was only half interested but that's a lot as far as females are concerned. He collared her for every dance and when he was excused during the excuse-me's he excused back without delay. Normally you'd give the round of the hall to the man who excused you but this man didn't allow him as far as the first corner.

The girl decided to make enquiries about the fellow in the cloakroom.

'What kind is your man?' she asked an acquaintance who chanced to be from the same townland. What she did not know was that this acquaintance was an extraordinary tale-carrier, totally incapable of transporting one iota of the truth even if her very life depended on it. She was, in short, a pathological liar and while her tales were never less than entertaining they were rarely based in fact and when they were itself, the truth was drowned in the flood of red lies which she manufactured on a non-stop basis.

'Your man is it?' she asked.

'Yes,' said the girl who had asked, 'your man.'

'If there was ten more of him there,' said the acquaintance, 'he wouldn't amount to one man.'

Disappointed, the unfortunate girl sought out confirmation. She asked a relative of the man who had been so attentive all night.

'I know nothing about him,' said the relative, 'except that his father was cashiered out of the Black and Tans.'

No wonder our friend had little time for Ballybunion. After hearing two such belittling descriptions the girl ignored him for the remainder of the dance.

But you wouldn't have to exaggerate to do damage to an innocent man or woman. What's that Alexander Pope said of his friend Addison:

Damn with faint praise, assent with civil leer
And without sneering teach the rest to sneer.

Of another friend he had this to say:

A wit with dunces
A dunce with wits.

Beware the tale-carrier, says the old maxim but is this quite fair! To destroy a man's character is, in a sense, to relieve him of his most valuable possession and does not the law always blame the receiver rather than the disposer. Therefore he who accepts the false account without demur is the real villain.

I was at a wake one night and I overheard two females talking about a third who had just knelt down to say a prayer for the repose of the soul of the corpse which lay on the bed. She bent her head and displayed a fine crop of curling, auburn hair.

'The bottle!' said the first female.

'A wig!' said the second. The wake room is a great

place for crucifying mourners. When they kneel they are bound to silence and they are exposed for all to see. Word of the woman's wig would soon be disseminated whether it was true or not. Indeed this is one of the many reasons why people attend wakes in the first place. They may spread scandal to their hearts' content and what harm, they say, if somebody gets hurt in the process! Are we not all in the world to be spoken about! Why should anyone be immune from scandal! Why speak about equality if one is not prepared to support it! Why be selective!

Another great place for spreading stories is the hospital bed. When two loquacious patients occupy neighbouring beds it is their entitlement to reveal titbits about their neighbours for the titillation of the ill and the indisposed.

I remember once a cousin of mine enquired about a neighbour of hers who happened to be married next door to the patient in the next bed. What my cousin heard was better than any tonic. Instead of being married into a place with fifty cows she had only married into nineteen. The farm was up to its hocks in debt and not rotting with money as my cousin had been led to believe. The patient in the next bed of course was exaggerating for she sensed that my cousin was interested only in a bad account of her former neighbour's circumstances. The patient was prepared to falsify the accounts on the grounds that my cousin needed cheering up and how better to cheer a person up than provide them with bad news about those who would rise above their station without any right to do so.

My cousin left the hospital a new woman. Even the doctor was mystified for his prognostications were all wrong. He had forecast a long stay and was happy to admit that he had diagnosed wrongly.

He hadn't. The cure lay in the news she heard, the distorted, unfair, untrue account of another's misfortune. No great harm came about as a result. The end, you might say, justified the means.

A Song with no Air

There is a quiet man who has, on rare occasions, adorned the corner opposite this place where I calefact my treatises. He is so quiet that even when the dogs piddle with disgusting frequency around the area where he stands he takes no notice, allowing the ill-mannered creatures to indulge themselves without fear of rebuke.

He is not a corner boy, not even a part time or temporary one. He is too self-effacing, too mild-mannered, too humble and too gentle by far to fill this most demanding of roles.

He calls to the corner once a week, bends his head deferentially if there is a resident corner boy and meekly allows his ample posterior to rest against the house front that forms part of the corner. Here he will remain for half an hour or so and the following is true. Witnesses will come forward to verify what I say if they are required by doubting Thomases to do so.

From the moment of his arrival to his departure the dogs which frequent the area, as I have already indicated, piddle without restraint all around his legs and sometimes on his shoes. Why the canines of my native town should select this humble representative of the human species for such outstanding honours is something I cannot explain. Is it his meekness and quietness that attracts them? He never shoos them away nor does he even take notice when they begin their relief work.

A neighbour told me lately that certain dogs are like that. They will retain their canine water until they find the right place to let it go. They will spend the morning foraging and fighting, growling and chasing motor-cars but the moment our man arrives they slink in his direction, survey him well and survey the scene thoroughly before raising legs aloft to indulge in their varying cascades.

Many are called, says the Good Book, but few are chosen. This man, however, has been chosen by the dogs of Listowel. These dogs are already notorious for soiling our streets and backways. The fruits of their labours are nearly always visible to strangers who stroll around the town. They are mystified. One German woman approached me one afternoon and asked me the following question: 'Deece are sacrit dogs no?'

'No!' I told her, 'they are very ordinary dogs.'

She expressed surprise and explained to some friends in her company that the dogs were not sacred. They also expressed surprise.

'Honely hin Hindia,' said she, 'haf I sin animals that soils de strits and deece are sacrit cows.' She departed after she had taken some photographs of the dogs and their droppings.

Let us return, however, to our quiet friend. Our friend is a man with a split personality but then who isn't when he has enough booze put away. Booze to the quiet man is what floodwaters are to the stranded fish, what the starting pistol is to the straining athlete, what the sound of the whistle is to the waiting midfielder.

The other night I had the privilege of beholding our meek friend in another role. There he stood outside my front door, his arms stretched wide, his head aloft and him singing a song to no particular tune. Granted he was sozzled to the very gills but I have seen other sozzled gentlemen who go home quietly and others still who kick doors, break windows and deliberately bump against offensive passers-by.

Despite the fact that the song had no air, it was not without words. These were of his own creation and I swear that I have never heard anything so complicated and so filled with long, hitherto-unheard phrases. It would take a Joycean scholar to unscramble the message contained therein.

What a change from the mild-mannered chap we saw standing at the corner less than twenty-four hours earlier with dogs piddling left, right and centre and him, half asleep, indifferent to their defilements.

His singing, if I may call it such, did not grate. Neither was it aggressive. It was soft and sweet as a summer breeze among the sallies of the river bank. He had his coat off and he sang to the passing cars. Some slowed to have a better look at him while others drove by lest he stumble across them. Let me say here that there wasn't a solitary dog in sight. A dog can always tell when a man is drunk. They have cause to know the difference between a sober master and a drunken master.

Our friend had now taken a break. He was holding up the front of my house and doing it admirably. His eyes had a faraway look and he slept for a period, opening bleary peepers occasionally in order to make sure that the world he knew so well was still to the good.

It was after the sleep that he proffered the piece-de-resistance of the evening. From his open mouth came a faint, high-pitched ululation the like of which you'd hear from an immature banshee. I have never heard an angel sing so I cannot make a comparison but I will say that our friend sang from the very depths of his soul. No sober man could sing the way he sang. The fact that he was drunk must not take away from the quality of his rendition. It was truly magnificent. It attracted the unstinted admiration of two small girls who, for a while, turned away from the cones they were licking to show their appreciation for the un-earthly sounds which assailed their young ears.

This was the cream, the essence of this drunken man's spirit, the very distillation of his purer being. I wished I had a recording device to record it for poster-ity. I was reminded of a country saying: you'll always meet the biggest bird the day you haven't got the gun.

Then the singing stopped and he wandered up-wards wiping his mouth with the back of his hand. There were different sounds now. He was crying. I left him to his grief and went indoors to tell my wife about the song I had heard. But how would I describe it? I would have to be a Shakespeare. It's there in *A Mid-summer Night's Dream*:

Since once I sat upon a promontory

44

And heard a mermaid on a dolphin's back
Uttering such dulcet and harmonious breath
That the rude sea grew civil at her song
And certain stars shot madly from their spheres
To hear the sea-maid's music.

Cuckooland

No cuckoo! It's the first year I've had to say this. He simply has not come. I have listened in vain evening after evening until the sun, often crimson, other times pink and shrouded sank into the bosom of the sea, six miles as the crow flies to the west of Dirha Bog.

He has been heard in other places by reliable listeners who know a cuckoo when they hear one. On the verge of Dirha Bog where I ramble most evenings it has often been his wont, since time immemorial, to announce his arrival as soon as he alighted on the green groves of Affoulia but this year he never showed up. He won't come now. The old people would tell you as much if they were here but they're not. They have all gone to England to be with their children or they have gone into the town where they will be safe from thieves and thugs who would callously wreck their lives.

Summer has come all right. One can see that in the bright meadows and greening hedgerows where other birds sing although none with the economy of our dusky Moroccan friend who never failed us before.

'Good riddance!' the mothers of the fledglings will say. 'Long enough he has taken over our abodes and callously evicted our young'.

They won't accept that the cuckoo simply follows nature's way which has to be cruel to be kind. In the bar, men shake their heads solemnly and say that the disappearance of the cuckoo from the green groves of Affoulia is only the beginning. Affoulia, they will tell you, is not the only place where the cuckoo has failed to fulfil his engagement. Townlands are reeled off: Bunagara, Skehenerin, Inchabawn, Shanahowen, Ballygoulogue.

'There was always a cuckoo in Glashnanaon,' one disgruntled seven cow farmer moaned, 'but 'tis three years now since he looked in on us.'

'I didn't hear a cuckoo since the missus died,' another man, a retired farmer, spoke from behind his pipe.

'What part of the world do you come from?' The question was posed by a woman who is forever on the lookout, so to speak, for a presentable man to whom she might minister legally on a permanent basis. She merely wanted to know if he lived near enough to a town or village before addressing herself seriously to his eventual capture.

'Tubbernagcuac.'

'Tubbernagcuac,' all present echoed. Not all understood that this was the Gaelic for the well of the cuckoos but most realised the awful significance therein.

'If,' said the seven cow farmer, 'he don't come to the spot which they named after him he'll come nowhere in the end.'

'In Knocknagoshel,' said the man with the pipe, 'there is a place called Glashnagcuac which means the stream of the cuckoo.'

'And does he still come?' asked the man from Tubbernagcuac.

47

'Oh he does but for how long more is the question.'

'I'm used to hearing the cuckoo all my life,' said the Tubbernagcuac man sadly, 'and when he don't show up I does be lonesome. Losing the wife was bad enough but losing the cuckoo on top of her is hard to take.'

There were murmurings of compassion. There wasn't a soul in the company who didn't commiserate in their hearts with the unfortunate creature from Tubbernagcuac.

One man invited him to have a drink but the astute woman forever in search of a likely man was the most sympathetic of all.

'Shove over here,' she said to him, "til I be telling you about the fine cuckoos we does have in my quarter of the world. Cuckoos,' said she chortlingly but con-fidentially, 'that does be cuckooing from morning till night in every kind of weather. Cuckoos that comes on time but don't always go on time so that you could be listening to them from one end of the summer to the other.'

The Tubbernagcuac man, being human, forsook the high stool where he had sat all morning and made his halting way to where she sat in a quiet corner where the comings and goings of cuckoos might be discreetly discussed till the day was down.

Addresses

People who are ashamed of their addresses should remember that Our Lord was born in a stable and people who are proud of their addresses should remember it even more.

The same applies to schools and families and all those who, by the grace of God, are possessed of attributes denied to others. The late Mickey Faulkner, true king of the road and ambassador to all known highways and by-ways, was a true travelling man. He once gave his address to a generous Yank who met him in these here licensed premises.

'Put down,' said he, 'Mickey Faulkner, Side of the Road, Ireland.'

'Will that find you for sure?' the Yank asked doubtfully.

'For sure,' Mickey assured him, 'unless I'm in jail or dead.'

There was another friend of mine who went forward for a job as a van salesman. All went well during the interview because my friend could talk the hind leg off a pot. He didn't get the job and he prevailed on me to ring up the firm, now folded and no surprise, in an effort to find out where he had gone wrong. Eventually I was put through to a decent sort of man who told me he'd ring me back. Time passed and he did.

'Well,' he said in a hesitant manner, 'it was his address, I believe.'

It transpired that it was the function of one of the interviewers to get in touch with a few reliable contacts in the town where my friend resided. Two of the contacts voiced the fact that they would have misgivings because of my friend's precise address. A third was wholeheartedly on my friend's side. As I have already stated he didn't get the job.

'Did these men come,' I asked the man on the phone, 'from a nearby address to the failed man or were they from a distant address?'

He confessed that they were from a distant address.

'But,' said I, 'why didn't you ask somebody from a nearby address and you would have received a more accurate and less biased account?'

'You stick to your plays,' he advised, 'and let us run our business our way.' I stuck to my plays and he ran his business his way. He wound up a disaster. I'm not surprised because his minions turned down one of the funniest men and best salesmen I ever knew.

I know the question you're going to pose now. What happened to the poor chap who was born in the wrong spot? He emigrated to London. He's doing all right. Not great, just all right.

What's the point of all this, my resident carpers are sure to ask and rightly so. I'm getting paid and well paid to elucidate, to simplify and to generally facilitate. I have not come here to waffle. Value for money is my motto. My theory is that if you give poor value the customer won't come back.

'Do you know who I am?' Dan Paddy O'Sullivan,

the great matchmaker once asked a pork butcher after he had given him fat chops instead of lean.

'No,' said the butcher.

'Behold,' said Dan, 'the man who won't come back.'

The moral is that there are no good addresses only good people. You can also be certain that there are more good people in so-called bad addresses than there are in so-called good addresses. This, in a way, is an apology to all the good men and women who have been discriminated against over the years by people with so-called good addresses.

I have not come here today to knock so-called good addresses. Be proud of your address wherever it is but don't parade it.

Barsounds

Oh for the touch of a vanished hand
And the sound of a voice that is still.

Tennyson

As a publican I often longed for stillness, sighed for it
in fact when the moon was riding high in the heavens
and the licensing laws were being breached. How is it I
would ask myself that men will insist on singing when
there are members of the garda síochána listening for
sounds of revelry in any and all taverns within earshot. How often have we heard a member of the force
speak as follows in a court of law: 'I heard voices my
Lord and when I investigated I found that there were
ten persons on the premises and that the publican
was filling pints.'

It's all there in that bald statement, man's un-
controllable desire for self-expression while the limbs
of the law are on the prowl.

It has been suggested that the animal is an inferior
species and yet you will never hear of a buffalo calf
mooing when the mountain lion is in the neighbourhood. Neither will you hear the lamb bleat when he
spots a fox. He'll find cover and lie low until the danger
passes. It's the same way with all hunted animals.
They will never advertise themselves when there's
danger. Only man, the allegedly most intelligent of all
creatures, does this. Even the wild ass will hold his

tongue when there are predators about and the ass is supposed to be thick.

The moon overhead sees all and makes no sound while beneath, infinitesimal man roars like a lion and crows like a cockerel, sings like a corncrake and hums like a hornet. Let him sing and let him roar but not when the minions of the law are on the lookout for after-hours drinkers.

Another oft-used expression in our courts of law used to be 'I heard the sounds of coins tinkling my Lord and when I inspected the premises I found seven on.'

In the old days when publicans depended for their livelihoods on after-hours drinking and while a cynical government pocketed the taxes derived therefrom a man who raised his voice in a public house after closing time placed the leisure time of his friends and neighbours in jeopardy. In no time at all he found himself without friends and with neighbours who eyed him with mistrust. Worse still he was no longer welcome in public houses either before or after hours. The last thing public house patrons want is a loud mouth. What then does one do when confronted with several loud mouths at the same time, loud mouths whose noisy and obscene laughter attracts the passing policeman the way light attracts a moth.

After-hours drinking, like the poor, we shall always have with us and no matter how strict the enforcement of the liquor laws they will not deter the thirsty night-soul or the business-hungry publican. There are even publicans who conduct their illicit businesses till the very crack of dawn and who are otherwise strong and perfect Christians. The just man falls seven times a day so why should not the poor publican fall once!

How I love stillness! However as much as I love it I also love a sing-song. What I do not love is the bawdy roar of the scoundrel who, unbidden, rends the silence of the peaceful night asunder and attracts the curious lawman who is often willing to leave well alone.

I remember one awful night in my after-hours heyday. The lights were dimmed and the pub was filled. Silence reigned and all that could be heard was the gentle sloshing of drink in pint and half pint glasses. There was the occasional smacking of appreciation after a particularly pleasant swallow had been negotiated. Outside the civic guards patrolled up and down but there was no danger to the pubs or to the inmates. What a happy hour it was. There was the element of risk to spice the taste of the booze and there was the unique camaraderie which exists wherever drinking men are foregathered.

Then came an unholy shriek from a man who poured a glass of gin into his whiskey instead of water. After the shriek he spluttered and apologised but it was too late. There came a loud knocking at the front door followed by a loud knocking at the back door. Both knocks were ones of authority. Only a policeman could knock in such wise. The pub was raided and names were taken. The man who shrieked was lucky not to have been hanged at least for his outburst.

There were many in that august assembly who never spoke to him again. I personally kept him outside my door for several years and only relented when his mother died. Everybody admitted after that disastrous raid that they were glad he wasn't hanged. Hanging, they said, was a decent way to die, they said, and he didn't deserve it.

Bringing Home the Drunk

There is no understanding so fraught with danger to the escort as the simple conveying home of a drunken man. Let the escort be a paragon of virtue, a pillar of the church, a most respected member of the community, it matters not a whit when he arrives at the home of the drunken man. The spouse of the incapacitated party, in such situations, cannot and will not see beyond her nose.

Upon beholding the innocent escort, nearly always a good samaritan within the true meaning of the word, the wife of the drunken man is instantly transformed into a raging she-devil, hell-bent on the destruction of the party who, out of the goodness of his heart, undertook to guide the alcoholically disabled man to his home.

My advice to you would-be benefactors in this respect is to convey the misfit to the vicinity of his home. Mark well the word vicinity. Under no circumstances convey him to the door itself. Dislodge him at least one door away from the one which is his. Prop him against the wall or better still seat him gently on his posterior with his back to a solid surface where he can come to no harm. Then draw breath as the man said and knock upon the fellow's door. Having executed a substantial knock withdraw as though you had deposited a lost lion cub at the entrance to its mother's den. In other words, run for your life.

I am not saying that all the spouses of deposited drunkards will turn upon the benefactor but it is an unfortunate fact of life that a substantial number will. This is why it is wise to take no chances. After the knock has been executed, vamooze. If the first knock is not answered keep making forays to the door, always making sure to remove yourself post haste after the door has been opened.

There are spouses who will invite the benefactor into the house, who will even offer him tea or other forms of liquid refreshment. I have encountered many such females myself and I have been overwhelmed with expressions of boundless gratitude. Indeed very often prayers and promises of prayers were showered upon me by the grateful spouse and I was deeply touched that my good deed was acknowledged.

However, it is definitely not worth the gamble. For every thankful spouse there is an unbeholden one as I have found out to my cost. Perilous as it is to convey home your drunken man it is tantamount to self-destruction to convey home a drunken woman. Men are more suspicious than women. They have less trust in their fellow men. Therefore if you are ever obliged to convey a drunken woman to her doorstep make sure you have another woman with you, drunken or otherwise.

Secondly it is well to remember that when you deposit your cargo it is vitally necessary to deposit the second woman as well. The minute the husband opens the door the sensible thing to do is to land him with both women. Let him, if the wretch has any conscience at all, convey the other woman home in return for your kindness to his spouse.

There are some other rules which should be observed in the conveying home of drunken men. Firstly, make sure that the drunken man is able to walk or, at least, partially walk. Never attempt to convey a drunken man home on your own. Thirdly make certain that his tie is loosened lest he choke himself. Fourthly, make sure he pukes before he reaches his own door. Drunken men have a nasty habit of depositing the contents of their stomachs on their doorsteps the moment the door is opened. Don't ask me why. Some observers have noted that a blast of heat from the warm interior of the house induces the puke in the drunken party. Others maintain that it is the sight of the wife often with hair curlers and without make-up. Whatever the reason it happens frequently.

Try to remember these elementary precepts and you will be well served. Finally the conveying home of drunken men is the responsibility of the companions with whom he has been drinking or, failing this, the function of the final publican on his drunken itinerary.

A Philosopher

A rare visit the other night from a philosopher who happens to be a relation of mine. His only other claim to fame, according to himself, is that he spent some time inside.

'A small matter of bigamy,' he would say cheerfully whenever anyone asked him why. Personally I think he was inside for something else altogether, something very ordinary because he has the mannerisms of a man not even married once not to mind twice. I can always tell whether a man is married or not by the look in his eyes, by the way he's dressed and by the way he carries himself.

'No, no, noo!' he shot back emphatically when I suggested that he was of the singular persuasion.

'I was married twice,' he insisted, 'and very nearly three times except that my luck ran out. My problem,' he continued breezily as is his wont, 'is that I was overheated sexually and could not resist females. I must have proposed to forty in my time.'

He went on to explain that only a quarter of that number accepted and he married only two for a number of reasons. When I asked him if he had learned anything from his marital experiences he answered that he learned not to take sides.

'When my two wives met before the court sat,' he informed us, 'they went at it hammer and tongs. I stayed mum and let 'em off until they exhausted themselves. If I had intervened it would only have made matters worse.'

After he had borrowed twenty pounds from me he repaid me instantly with the following advice.

'When there's big trouble,' said he, 'like relations sounding off or in-laws or even war just find a place that isn't a side and sit it out. If someone offers you a side out of the goodness of their hearts make sure you decline.'

He accepted a small whiskey from a freshly-converted admirer who required more knowledge about sex.

'I'm too old for sex now,' he explained. 'I often thought about getting rid of my penis or donating it but I decided against it so I hang on to it for its sentimental value.'

Here now was a true philosopher with a detached view which is the hallmark of the philosopher everywhere.

His questioner, alas, did not see him in this light and took umbrage at the answer suggesting that it was facile and that the philosopher was not really a philosopher at all but a fool.

'I know what I am,' he said, 'which is more than can be said for you. You must be close on forty years and here you are still asking questions about sex.'

Here the philosopher became heated.

'The secret of sex,' said he, 'is not to take it seriously. That's your problem. Sex is a funny business, not a serious one.' So saying he produced a broken pocket comb from his trousers pocket and proceeded to decorate himself taking advantage of the bar mirror. The man who had been rebuked fumed and would have resorted to physical redress had not the philosopher elaborated.

'Your trouble is that you probably go back with old girlfriends which is fatal, fatal for you my friend and fatal for the old girlfriends who hang around waiting instead of seeking fresh fields and pastures new. I never returned to abandoned girlfriends. Why pester them when you can provide them with freedom. Why shackle yourself with ancient things when you might sup afresh in a world that's forever throwing up beautiful women, consenting women and indeed all kinds of women. Why settle for one when you might have a pair. Take my advice my friend and address yourself this very night to fresh females.'

The man to whom he presented his philosophising didn't know whether to choke him or smite him. In the end he paid his fee of a half a one and a pint. Later he would confess to me that he proposed to a new woman that very night and did not suffer the instant rebuff he expected.

'Ask me again,' she advised him, 'when I'm in better humour.'

Unfortunately philosophers are not always appreciated especially in public houses. People who regularly visit pubs, in the first place, are generally somewhat confused when philosophised at. The confusion which was already there to begin with because of alcoholic intake becomes compounded. Confusion begets annoyance and annoyance begets anger and anger begets blows and nearly always the philosopher is a sensitive chap, very often underdeveloped so that he becomes a prime target for the drunken buck who is already halfway on the high road to full-scale thuggery. Misapplied philosophy simply completes the journey for him.

Since philosophers do not hunt in packs, they are without recourse to protection. Since they are always reactionaries lacking in diplomatic skills they are the natural prey of the drunken thug in which this unfortunate country of ours abounds just now. When philosophers are struck down and they frequently are there is no outcry. Most tramps are philosophers of a kind and are easy meat for gangs of bully-boys.

But let us return to our very own philosopher. His face bears the scars of several beatings. He might have avoided this painful punitive action if he had left a few balls over the bar and kept his own counsel but philosophers are not made this way, especially bankrupt ones who have spent periods in jail. They must entertain if they are to sample the produce of the public house.

'I know what fear is,' he told us, 'but I do not live in fear.'

We asked him if he feared anything. He pondered a while before answering.

'The knife,' he said bitterly, 'the pale, pale knife, third hand of the coward.'

'The most beautiful woman I ever saw was a golf club tease,' he told us when we asked him about beautiful women. 'She had the longest, brownest legs I ever saw and the most curvaceous body but she was of no use to anybody. That was in my heyday when I had things going for me. She was there to tease not to please. She reminded me of a distant mountain with snow at its summit, totally unassailable and with a refrigerated dislike for predatory philosophers like myself.'

Alive or Dead

This very day I received a letter from a young lady in Wexford informing me that she never realised I was alive. She has some books to be autographed and would like to bring them to be signed some time.

Only last week I received a letter from a girl in County Longford who has a part in the local production of one of my plays. She writes towards the end of the letter: 'I'm sorry to have to say this but I didn't know you were still alive till I heard you were dead'.

All I can say to these miscalculations, totally innocent of course, is that I am happy to announce my aliveness to all and sundry and my availability as an answerer of letters. At least I think I'm alive or maybe I'm in a dream! The late Joe Quaid who resided on the slopes of fabled Knockadirreen near the village of Duagh used always say that a man had no way of knowing he was dead until there was a headstone over him. Joe, of course, was originally a native of Dirreen Athea which once abounded in poets.

Joe once told me that Athea had the only goat butcher in Ireland. He sold only whole goats and half goats. Of the half he sold, one half carried the tail and the other no tail at all. The half with the tail, according to Joe, sold at sixpence while the half with no tail sold at five pence.

Apparently the tail of a goat had no equal in the making of soup. Anyway, be that as it may, Joe had a preoccupation with headstones and the inscriptions thereon. His favourite was one which I once personally saw in the English midlands some miles to the east of Northampton. It went like this:

Here lies poor Fred
Who was alive and is dead.
If it was his brother
That would have been another.
If it was his sister
Nobody would have missed her
But since it was poor Fred
Who was alive and is dead
There's no more to be said.

Joe himself was presumed dead after he collapsed under a large sheet of hardboard on his way out of McKenna's mill here in this very town whose very streets and backways I walk every day and sometimes night. All Joe did was faint but some of the town's numerous exaggerators, and we have plenty, sent out word that he was dead. The upshot of the sorry business was that Joe received several mass cards or rather his next-of-kin received them.

Regarding my own supposed extinction I have never felt more alive than I do at this moment. In fact the captious old midwife who brought me into the world announced to my father that I would live to be a ripe old age if drink didn't get the better of me prematurely. It has been touch and go for many a long day now. You might say I'm just ahead of the posse. The bother is that this particular posse catches up

65

with everybody sooner or later.

I have never, thanks be to God, been described as being dead and alive. I don't think I could stand that although one might think that by now I have become immune to criticism.

One balmy evening in July of this year, after returning from a riverside stroll, I sat myself down on my favourite stool outside the bar counter and treated myself to a pint. As I sat imbibing at my leisure, a good-looking girl, from Mayo it transpired later, sat down beside me. She noticed a painting of yours truly on the wall behind her.

'Is he long dead now?' she asked the girl behind the counter.

'A good bit now,' she answered, 'although you couldn't trust him. He could reappear at any moment.'

The visitor swallowed a little from her lager and addressed herself to me.

'What got him in the end?' she asked.

'I wish I knew,' I told her truthfully, adding to myself that it was just as well I could not forecast what I might eventually pass on from because there's no doubt whatsoever if it wasn't one thing it would most certainly be another.

It's a strange feeling, knowing that others believe you to be dead. I dreamed I was dead once and that I wound up in after-life in Ballylongford seated in a crowded public house. There was a rousing sing-song in progress. I asked myself, during that sojourn, if maybe Ballylongford was heaven. When I woke up I realised it was a dream and that I had been the subject of wishful thinking.

Worse was to follow. Some days later a busload of Yanks arrived. I was in the bar at the time and since they did not know me from the paintings and photographs in the bar I felt that I was genuinely dead. Even the courier who was Irish believed me to be dead too. The missus who stood behind the counter awaiting their instructions booze-wise waited in vain for the purchase of drink was the last thought in their heads. All they wanted was a souvenir of the deceased or of the premises. What they really wanted was a free book each. They seemed genuinely surprised, even aggrieved, when no such commodity was forthcoming. One became truculent but the situation was saved by a Corkman who resides now in this part of the world. He intervened and in the most polite manner imaginable provided them with directions to the local cemetery and the exact location of my grave.

There's no week passes but some visitor asks whether I'm alive or dead.

'He was alive and dead,' said a local GAA official, 'when he was playing football.'

Even elderly people pose the question: 'Is he long dead now?' My missus who is a truthful soul tells them that I am alive and well but this has the effect of making them shake their heads in disbelief.

On another occasion a bus-load of Clare people were divided as to whether I was dead or alive. One of the party, a gentleman with a piano accordion, solved the problem to some extent.

'I remember that fella writing for the *Leader*,' said

the man, 'when I was on the run from the Tans.'

The question remains as to whether I'm worth more alive or dead. That will not be resolved in this place and at this time but I will be spoken highly of, not because of any claim I might have, but because it is the fashion never to say a bad word about the dead.

I must be the only man in this part of the world who knows how Lazarus felt when he was raised from the dead. I have been consigned to the dead and I have risen. I rose this morning at twenty past nine and it is my fond hope that I will rise for many a morning yet D.V.

Canavan and Callaghan

Readers will long be familiar with the sayings and doings of the Prophet Callaghan who was so called because he was fond of referring to the Good Book whenever he found himself in an impasse.

He had a worthy foil in the late Sonny Canavan, his lifelong friend. That would be the same Canavan of the goats and the talking dog, the same Canavan who was many times King of the Wrenboys and whose passing left this part of the world a duller place.

The pair were one day cutting turf in Dirha Bog with a third party who employed them for the day. Then, as now, turf-cutters had to go signing before starting the day. No, no, not autographs but the dole.

The man who employed the pair was a deeply religious man and like all religious folk he never wronged anybody whenever possible and never, ever wronged himself. Towards the end of eight hours constant endeavours Canavan announced to his employer that it had been a long day. That worthy made no comment but diligently piked up the turf which Callaghan cut with his slean in the boghole several feet below.

After a half hour Canavan spoke secondly.

'It will be dark soon,' said he.

'It will be dark every night,' said his immovable employer.

After another half hour Canavan spoke again.

'If we don't stop soon the pubs will be shut,' said

he.

'They does shut every night,' said his religious employer. Then a great, booming voice came from the boghole. It was the Prophet Callaghan whose body had grown numb from his labours. He relied upon the psalms as was frequently his wont. Suddenly came his anguished cry: 'Up from the depths I have cried to Thee, Lord; Lord hear my voice!'

His voice was heard for almost immediately his employer called a halt to the work. Reluctantly he paid both labourers their wages. He feared the wrath of the Lord.

'I have fought a good fight,' said Callaghan. 'I have finished the course. I have kept the faith.'

'But what profit it a man if he gain the whole world and the pubs be closed,' said Canavan

'Be sober, be vigilant,' cautioned Callaghan, 'for the devil goes about as a roaring lion seeking whom he may devour.'

'Does he ever think about anything but pubs?' his employer asked Callaghan.

'Better for him,' said Callaghan, 'that a millstone be tied around his neck and that he be cast into the depths of the bog hole.'

The employer was impressed and when Callaghan asked him for an advance of a half a crown for himself and his friend against the following day's wages he reluctantly acquiesced. Callaghan knelt before his benefactor and loudly prayed for him and if he had an appropriate garment he would verily have kissed its hem.

Later on the road to Listowel Canavan accused

Callaghan of servitude beyond the call of duty. Callaghan found his answer in Matthew.

'Whoever exalteth himself shall be abased,' said he, 'but he that humbleth himself shall be exalted.'

Canavan could only shake his head in admiration.

Later that night in Mickey Corridan's pub in Market Street they sat quaffing pints of stout as only bogmen can quaff. Mickey Corridan joined them after a while.

'See how filled with humility I am,' said Callaghan.

'How do you make that out?' asked Canavan.

'Doth I not drink with publicans and sinners?' Callaghan asked in return, quoting from Apocrypha.

'Ye'll have to talk low,' said Mickey Corridan. 'I saw a sergeant and two guards in the street earlier tonight.'

'And in the year that King Uzzah died,' said Callaghan, 'I saw also the Lord sitting upon a throne. Above it stood the Seraphims; each one had six wings. With twain he covered his face and with twain he did fly.'

Mickey Corridan who had an ear for poetry bought the pair a round of drinks.

'For my sins,' said he.

'For all our sins,' said Callaghan.

And it so happened that the stars withdrew from the heavens and that the bright light of the dawn danced in the eastern world and all the pubs in Listowel discharged their motley crews and the cocks crowed in the western lands. Nevertheless Canavan and Callaghan arrived at the bog in time and set to work with a will so that their employer raised his eyes aloft to the heavens and thanked God that just men

71

still inhabited the world.

The hours went by. Food was brought by the wife of the employer and soon the day was all but down.

'It will be dark soon,' said Callaghan.

'When it isn't bright, it's dark,' said his employer. Canavan said no more for from the depths of the bog hole came the booming voice of the Prophet Callaghan. This time he resorted to Genesis for he had burst blisters upon his palms and there was blood on them.

'Whosoever sheddeth man's blood,' he cried out, 'by man shall his blood be shed.'

The employer gave the order to halt at once thinking that his life might be in danger.

It was then that Callaghan asked him for an advance but it was pointed out to him that all the turf was cut and that their services would not be required until the following year.

'And who says that any of us will be there this time next year,' said the employer. He then went on to speak about life's uncertainty and about rash promises until Callaghan grew tired of it all.

From Maccabbees he did quote: 'It is a foolish thing,' said he, 'to deliver a long prologue and be short in the story itself.'

The employer said no more. He gathered his implements and girded his loins. He tackled his ass to the cart.

'Thou art weighed in the balance,' said he to Callaghan, 'and thou art found wanting. Giddy up ass and be gone.'

Write a Book

I think every man and every woman should write a book before it's too late. Even if it's not published it could be left there to be perused by anybody who might come along. The book need not be about one's own life. It could be about another's as seen through the eyes of the writer. This way we will know more about the writer for writers are merely hazy reflections of those about whom they write.

It's an awful waste to see a life that's been lived to the full being lowered into the grave without a record remaining. My mother and, indeed your mother dear reader, had more in her head than most who write books but yet they never wrote.

'Who? Me?' they would be sure to respond if asked to write a book. Yet they had true wisdom and humour and charity and when they had almost lived out a life they also had the great age that overflows with the sagacity that comes from experience.

I had aunts and uncles and cousins and neighbours with mighty stories to tell about themselves and others but such was their humility and fear of ridicule that they preferred to leave silently without a testament, a testament which might have saddened or cheered, weakened or sustained. No matter what, it would be a record of one person against his or her background, a listing of events important and unimportant and if they are unimportant itself remember

73

that what might seem unimportant to one person might be momentous to someone else.

It's important that you, dear reader, should tell your tale from beginning to end.

'Yours,' you might say, 'is no different to any other human tale,' but there you would be so wrong, for yours, while being alike to others, is quite unique. Yours has freckles and flecks and hues and joys and sorrows like no other. All right, all right. Maybe it's true that all lives are taken from the same pattern but this should make no difference for it is the embellishment of your personal experiences and interpretations that will make the book different from others.

It's an awful shame that men should die filled with untapped wisdom and knowledge, a shame that they should fade away with no one benefiting from their stores of agony and grief and suffering, from the sum of their experiences in the journey from cradle to grave.

There's a book in everyone. It's not necessary that your book should be published and if you can't write it yourself you should allow it to be drawn out of you by somebody else. This will do you the world of good because afterwards the world, as you know it (the northern or maybe the southern portion of the parish) will have a fuller understanding of you and many things about you will be explained in a way that is not possible by merely expiring silently with the whole secret of your life locked up within you and the whole complicated and monumental tale on its way to total decay for bones don't speak and dust is silent too.

You owe it to your neighbours to write a book, to your friends and to your enemies, to your children and to your grandchildren. What good is money if it cannot be spent. In the same way what good is knowledge if it cannot be passed on. By knowledge I mean the good and the bad experiences that will help those that you are leaving behind. The book is there, inside you, in your face and in your hands and in your heart and mind.

I once asked Davy Gunn, the bodhrán-maker, if he would write an account of his life but he said no. I asked him if he would allow someone else to write an account of his life and he told me that I was always writing about him and that was enough.

'Anyway,' said he, 'the whole truth cannot be told about any man and must never be told.'

'But,' I said, 'the whole truth is so well known to all that it doesn't matter. It's so inherent in us that it goes without saying, the bodily functions, the notions, the lunacies. These are so much a part of us that you would only bore your readers or maybe disgust them by adhering to such mundane, everyday balderdash.'

'It's all in my face and in my hands,' Sonny Canavan told me when I said he should record his life from start to finish.

'Wouldn't you like to know what people think about you after they hear your story?' I asked.

'What I'd like,' said Canavan, 'is to know what my goats think about me. Now that's something. What do the dogs think about me and the birds?'

Those of you who have come this far with me might

be induced by what you have read up to this to consider writing a book. If you have a few scores or more of years put behind you there has to be the makings of a book. I knew a man in Listowel who wrote to his daughter before he died. In the letter he told her he loved her and that he was leaving her all he had. Then in a postscript he wrote 'I was'.

He was wrong. He still is in her memory and indeed in mine because I liked the man and sincerely miss him. He was a despondent fellow in life but this, I feel, was because he did not think enough of himself. I knew nothing about his personal life or of his experiences. All I knew about him was that he stood his round and went to Mass regularly, that he had a hot temper which cooled instantly and that he had two songs which he sometimes sang, 'Shenandoah' and 'The Black Hills of Dakota'.

I didn't know enough about him and that's not fair. I should have been privy to more if only to satisfy my curiosity. I feel deprived because I liked and enjoyed him and his ways. Now if he had written a book I would know a lot more about him and indeed I honestly feel that this is my entitlement. When I spoke to his daughter she agreed that he had a book in him for when she was young and when he'd be drunk he would spin for her romantic tales about himself during his journey through the world. At least he left her fragments of what might have been a book. He left the rest of us nothing.

So, dear reader, take your friends and those who love you or even hate you into account and start somewhere on your own or with the help of others.

Don't delay. Put it down bit by bit and in no time at all you will have a worthwhile testament to leave behind you.

Waiting for Tuesday

I have come to the conclusion lately that one spends one's life fruitlessly unless we prod ourselves into awareness at every possible opportunity, unless we remind ourselves that there is more to life than ourselves and our problems.

As I walked around my native town on Monday afternoon last I met a man walking around the town's spacious square. He was a well-dressed chap, affluent and reasonably affable. As we drew nearer each other I recognised him. In fact he had been at the local school with me although a few years my junior. We spoke of many things, dead teachers, departed colleagues, local and national scandals and, of course, Kerry football.

'It appears to me,' he said before we were about to part, 'that ye spend Monday in Listowel waiting for Tuesday.'

There was a time when I would have reacted angrily but the years have imposed their restraints and I am no longer as impulsive as I was.

'Don't you agree?' he said.

I didn't respond at once. I gave him his head so to speak. I find that if we tighten the reins or even skimp we prematurely subdue important revelations.

'I mean,' he continued, 'there's nothing happening and I mean nothing. There isn't a Christian on the streets and even the traffic's non-existent.'

This wasn't strictly true. I am a Christian and so

were three other people in the vicinity. We might not be perfect Christians but I'm sure we bend over backwards trying, often fruitlessly. There was plenty of traffic, at least plenty for me. Two lorries had just passed and they even drowned out our talk for a while.

The real problem with Listowel on Monday is that it's the weekly half-day. Most of the shops are closed and those who can go driving to Tralee. If the day is fine they go to Ballybunion. There used to be a shopkeeper in Listowel in my hey day who maintained that Listowel people would sooner shop in hell than in Listowel.

'Go to Tralee of a Monday,' he used to say, 'and you'll see more Listowel people than Tralee people there.'

That may well be but it also may well be that they're not all shopping. Anyway, half-days tend to be quiet in small towns and I know some places that are positively eerie when the half-day comes round. Then there are other lifeless spots where ordinary days and half-days are indistinguishable.

Personally speaking my wife and I may be seen in Abbeyfeale on most Mondays. No. We don't stop there except to buy a few pounds of home-cured bacon. What we do is take off at about three o'clock and motor to Athea over tree-lined, lovely roads and from there we go to Abbeyfeale and thence to the Parson's Cross near Feale Bridge. From there we journey on towards Derrindaffe and Listowel. It's a change of scene and the vistas, while not spectacular, are pleasing to the eye. There is no monotony in these excursions. We take note of the progress of houses under construction, wonder at the deepening green of the fields and of the overhanging trees, comment on the state of the many streams and rivers over which we pass and return to Listowel around five o'clock, just in time to prepare the dinner.

To return, however, to my friend who said that we spend Monday in Listowel waiting for Tuesday, I suggested to him after he seemed to have run out of steam that all towns need a rest from the hustle and bustle of the week. I pointed out that it provided perceptive Listowel people with the chance to inspect the streets, the town park, the river and the town square which is what I do while the missus is preparing the dinner. I also told our friend that when I was much younger we would take advantage of the half-day to visit public houses which were not our locals. At that time the town had seventy public houses against forty-seven now.

There was the danger that we might never see the interiors of those interesting and friendly premises if we did not avail of our half-days to do so. There were, for instance, several which never indulged in after-hours trade, believe it or not, and there were others still where young chaps were courteously discouraged at night but not by day. The regulars in these preserved establishments were nearly all middle-aged or senile and they found the presence of youth disruptive. Their sedentary ways, and these were their entitlement, would shrivel before the advent of noisy youth.

But for the half-day we would never get to know those other public houses and the many interesting inmates who hung their coats there.

Monday was also a day when old people came out of doors. I spoke to an old woman lately.

'It's safer,' she confided, 'and there's two supermarkets open. I can go for a stroll and visit the church. I can even cross the road because there's hardly any traffic. Oh I love Monday,' she concluded blissfully, 'it's my favourite day of the week.'

So we see gentle reader that half-days can mean different things to different people.

In all towns changes take place imperceptibly so that if one wishes to find out what goes on it is imperative to use some portion of our half-days in order to fill ourselves in. Maybe the developments might not appeal to all the town's inhabitants. For this reason one should regularly traverse the lesser as well as the larger areas. One should inspect everything and anything in the interest of one's town and its inhabitants, the majority of whom leave it to others to say things that should be said and do things that should be done.

The ideal starting point for a walk that could be instructive as well as pleasing to the eye and relaxing to the body is from your own front door or back door and from there to the town park entrance, then around by Gurtenard by the banks of the Feale before setting back for home.

Before I parted with our friend who claimed we were waiting for Tuesday I told him there is no one who is not waiting for something else. If we hadn't something to wait for we would all expire from depression.

A Horsechestra

'I'd swear if I was asked,' said Henry, 'I 'eard a horse-chestra.' Henry was my English landlord and he made the remark as we walked through the park in North-ampton. Sure enough, after we had listened a while, there came the strains of a brass band and in no time at all it was upon us with drum, cymbal and French horn.

'Hoi was right,' said Henry. 'Hit was a horseches-tra.' There chanced to be a third party with us at the time and he nudged me rather forcibly, winking con-spiratorially as he did at Henry's mention of the horse-chestra.

Later in the pub he told me in an aside that he thought Henry first meant there were some horses in the vicinity.

'Not so,' I informed the fellow as curtly as I could without offending him, 'for if Henry had meant that there were horses neighing or whatever in the vicinity he would have said "I 'ear 'orses neighin'."'

Another day we were leaving the church after a particularly gruelling sermon from an elderly priest who covered the same ground several times over the space of thirty-five minutes. We tended to be critical as we moved away from the church in the general direc-tion of the neighbourhood's hostelries.

'Naw, naw!' said Henry emphatically, "im be all right, 'im be upliftin' in 'is way.'

"Ymn!' said the same man who had spoken in the pub after the horsechestra's appearance, 'what hymn! I didn't hear any hymn.'

'Neither did I,' I returned bitingly.

'Wot's he on about now?' Henry asked.

'He says he didn't hear any hymn,' I informed Henry.

"E didn't 'ear no 'ymn,' said Henry dismissively, "cos there werrint no 'ymn.'

Henry was not of our persuasion but he came along on Sundays out of respect. Since we shared the same pub in the church's vicinity he decided that it couldn't do any harm if we shared the same church. Feeling that he might have been a trifle abrupt with our friend he placed a hand on his shoulder and asked him gently 'wot 'ymns you like then lad?'

Mystified, the young man addressed himself to me. He spoke in a whisper.

'Will you tell him,' said he, 'that I am not a hymn-lover, that if I was asked to sing a hymn to save my life I couldn't do so.'

"Im that don't 'ave no 'ymn,' said Henry, at his most apocalyptic now, 'be askin' for it.'

'Asking for what?' my friend asked as mystified as ever.

'Look at it like this mate.' Henry laid a paternal hand on his shoulder for the second time. 'Suppose the life rafts was all agone. Wot was we gonna do if we didn't 'ave no 'ymn? Answer me that mate!'

No answer was forthcoming. It would be some time before our friend accepted the fact that Henry had his way of saying things and that all one had to do was come to terms with this.

'If I 'ad a rum for every 'ymn I sung at sea,' Henry shook his head, 'I reckon as 'ow I'd fill a fair-sized pond.'

Then there was the time of the ham. Henry's wife Beryl had gone for her annual weekend to her only remaining relative in Hull. We were left to fend for ourselves. We consumed only half the food we normally would but we balanced the books as it were by consuming twice the amount of beer or in 'enry's case three times the amount.

We decided to forego lunches over the weekend. We had sizable reserves of fat built up over the spring and early summer and anyway as Henry was fond of pointing out it was "an 'orrible waste of drinkin' time.'

'Oose 'avin' 'am?' Henry asked as he proceeded to cover our plates with cold meat at Sunday supper.

'That isn't ham but I'll have some,' said my friend. Now we all knew it wasn't ham. Meat was rationed at the time but it was as near to ham as one could get in the post war period.

'It's more 'am than not,' Henry countered and slapped several slices on to each of our plates.

'Hoime hunhappy.' Henry paused with a forkful of the artificial ham an inch from his mouth.

What he was really trying to intimate was that he missed Beryl.

"Ere!' He turned on my friend, "ave my 'am,' and with that he placed two untouched slices on my friend's plate.

'You're sure?' asked my friend.

'Hoi ham. Hoi ham,' Henry assured him.

We finished the meal in silence as Henry's eyes moistened with memories of Beryl.

'She'll be home tomorrow,' we consoled him.

He cheered up at once.

"Ome tomorrow!' he clapped his hands. "Am today!' and so saying he recovered his ham from my friend's plate and gobbled it down like a hound for he had no breakfast and he had no lunch. He had only beer.

"Im be awright!' He pointed at my friend.

'Oh go on then,' said he, 'sing a hymn if you must.'

Henry needed no second bidding. It could be said that he was ripe for song. He had a broken baritone with a nice froth on it:

Nearer, my God to thee
Nearer to thee!
E'en though it be a cross
That raises me.

We succeeded in stopping him eventually when we managed to get it through to him that the pubs would be in danger of closing.

'Bloody 'ell!' he said. 'Bloody 'ell an' all!' A horrified look appeared on his good-natured face. He lifted his cap from its peg. We followed him out on to the bright street, lit by a full moon. He sang:

Rock of ages, cleft for me,
Let me hide myself in Thee.

Then and only then did he notice the moon.

"Im be awright,' he said, "im be awright.'

Rejection

To be rejected by a female is merely to be seasoned for a second assault upon the citadel of romance. We've all heard how the stone rejected by the builder became the corner stone. According to a farmer friend the same applies to bulls. I know. I know I've written about rejected bulls for years but, this time out, I am writing about rejection generally.

There was a footballer one time who could not get a place in the Knocknagoorley junior football team and he wound up playing for Kerry. We must not blame the Knocknagoorley selection committee for overlooking our friend for he may have been no more than a gangly apprentice at the time. How often does the misshapen sapling turn out to be the regal oak which stands broader and taller than any of its companions! Eh!

How often were my own works rejected for one reason or another and yet at the end of the day they survive! I blame nobody. Rather do I blame the time, the place and the circumstance for by such matters are we governed. Then, if our star is not in the ascendancey, we may be left stranded or as Shakespeare said: 'All the tides of our lives will be bound in shallows and in miseries'. I may not have it exactly right but then I tend to take liberties with the great bard for, as many of you will know, Shakepeare's mother came from a townland between Tarbert and Listowel and would be, so to speak, a neighbour and what are neighbours for, I ask you, but to be used as we see fit!

Then look at all the rejected songs and singers. How long did it take for them to truly surface and take their rightful places on the world stage!

Look at the great cooks who couldn't boil an egg when they were young and who, later in the day as it were, watered the mouths of countless monarchies. Then mourn for those who never made it, who never got the breaks. How's that Thomas Gray puts it:

Full many a gem of purest ray serene
The dark unfathomed caves of ocean bear.
Full many a flower was born to blush unseen
And waste its sweetness on the desert air.

Then look at all the good footballers who came on stream during the reign of Kerry's greatest football fifteen. They were good but not good enough. They would have been good enough any other time except the time they appeared. They were destined never to star.

Rejection my friends is no joke. It can set a man back upon his heels and leave him in a position from which he'll never recover.

There is only one situation where rejection can be an advantage. I speak, as if you hadn't guessed, about our friend the rejected lover. I have always maintained that only a lover who has been rejected not once but several times will attain to the very highest pinnacle of his profession.

I was first rejected by a red-haired cailín in the Pavilion Ballroom in Ballybunion in the year 1945. She would have been three or four years older and it could well be that I did not represent a sound investment for her time and attention. She would be on the look-out for a marriageable chap with a steady job. I was still a schoolboy and a steady job was nowhere on the horizon. My friends told me at the time that I had aimed too high, that I should have gone after somebody of my own age who was less attractive than the beautiful redhead. I refused to lower my sights, however, and went after a second mature partner. I was scoffed at by the object of my desires. A lesser soul would have wilted but I was imbued with a reckless courage which came from my Stacks Mountains ancestors.

Third time lucky. I approached and was warmly received by a brunette of about twenty-four. Of course she would dance with me. Why wouldn't she! We waltzed and we exchanged confidences. When the dance was over she handed me her purse to mind.

'It will only be in my way,' she explained, 'while I'm looking for my future husband. You have an honest face,' she said, 'and you won't run away with it.'

It was total rejection no matter what way one looks at it. I was consigned to the role of purse-minder rather than woman-minder. Time passed and I would escort many girls home from dances. Other times I would be outdone, out-foxed and outdanced not by the obvious Casanovas, the loudmouths, the loud dressers, the show-off dancers but by the sly ones, the self-effacing chaps who said little or danced little or indeed who did not look like real opposition.

I am reminded of that great writer Malcolm Lowry. How did he put it again: 'How many patterns of life are based on kindred misconceptions. How many wolves do we feel on our heels while our real enemies go in sheepskins by.'

I have often felt that it must be terrible for a man to have never been rejected by a woman, to be always acceptable whilst the ordinary mortal must suffer his share before he matures to manhood or to an age where rejection matters not a whit. To be old and not to have been rejected must surely be an unbearable situation. Whilst most of us ponder on what might have been the unrejected man has no cud to chew. How the blazes can you enjoy success if you have never tasted failure! How can you attain to perfection if you haven't gone through the furnaces of rejection!

I knew a man who went to Mass every morning of his life in total thanksgiving for a rejection which changed his life. There he was, infatuated by a beautiful woman in his own street. Not a minute passed that he did not think about her.

'I must whip up,' said he, quoting our friend Shakespeare again, 'my courage to the sticking point.'

Then came a summertime dance. She was there in all her glory, dressed in dark green which perfectly matched her eyes. He invited her to dance and she gladly accepted. He was a presentable chap with a steady job. It certainly would not be beyond him to maintain a female in the style to which she had become accustomed. Later, after he had danced with her three times in all, he asked her if it would be all right to see her home. She replied in the negative. Not to be out-done he asked again and upon being rejected asked a final time. She made it clear that she was not interested.

Some months later she married a man from out of town. She broke his melt as the saying goes and he endured a life of sorrow and suffering throughout their marriage.

Our friend who had been rejected was so delighted that he was not the victim, he underwent a change for the better. He married a plain Jane but she made him happy and that's all that matters in the end, that and the grace of God.

Smiles

There's nothing like a smile. It cheers and it uplifts and it's contagious, generally speaking that is. We had a teacher once who had a set on a certain pupil. As pupils go he was as big a blackguard as the next but he was no worse than that.

Unfortunately for him he always wore a smile except that it wasn't quite a smile. It had nuances of sniggers, grins and slyness and it was fixed. It was quite an irritating fixture and I must say that I sometimes found it quite annoying although it's proprietor and I were friends. Its permanence was the poor fellow's undoing.

One day the teacher stood on a rickety chair as he endeavoured to open a window which prohibited the inflow of fresh air into a congested classroom. Teacher or no, his equilibrium played second fiddle to the unpredictable motions of the chair and he fell off. As he lay on the floor cursing his ill-luck the first thing he noticed was the smile on the face of the pupil who had always sported the smile to begin with. The teacher rose, mouthed a classical obscenity and, in the heat of the moment, soundly slapped the grinning face which had infuriated him.

Weeks would pass before he realised that the smile was an invariant as they say in mathematical circles. It was a new class that had yet to impose itself on the teacher's susceptibilities. In the course of time all would be revealed but each side would have to suffer its share before that happened. The class also contained a chronic wheezer and it took the teacher weeks to establish the fact that the wheezes were authentic.

There were two snifflers in the class and one cougher. They were rasping coughs, grating on the ear but the poor chap had a sensitive tonsil and that was that.

There was one grinner and there was one sad face, so sad that it seemed its proprietor was about to break out in a fit of sobbing at any moment. He never did but the possibility existed.

There was one frowning face. This chap never smiled. The frown was as permanent as the ceiling overhead was unchanging. I am sorry to have to say that in the last analysis it proved a more valuable asset than the permanent smile.

When the teacher discovered that the smile was a fixture he tried to atone for the slap he had so unjustly administered but the only acknowledgement he received was the same unchanging smile. This irritated him no end as he was later to confess to me when I was man enough to drink a pint with him. He managed to conceal his irritation however and for this he must be accorded considerable credit. This teacher had no problems with the pupil who wore the perpetual frown or with the wheezer or the cougher or the sniffler once he got used to them but he could never get used to the smiler no matter how hard he tried. Go back now, if you will, gentle reader and see if you don't recall similar smilers who were the author's of their own misfortunes as well as their teacher's disgruntlement.

I met this particular smiler recently and he hadn't changed. He brought the smile from his mother who worked as shop assistant here in Listowel before she married. She too was possessed of a permanent smile but hers was acquired whereas her son was born with it. The first day she went to work her mother had warned her to have a smile for everybody. She had but alas she also had a smile for those who imparted news of personal disasters. These confidences should have been greeted with sympathy and even tears but never with smiles.

As her son began to emerge from toddlerhood she saw that he had an inbuilt smile which was fine up to a point but far from perfect in that it could frequently irritate.

So we see gentle reader that much as the smile is to be admired and appreciated there is also a time and a place for it.

A Personal Tramp

I'm a lucky man in that I have my own personal tramp. He has, more or less, adopted me. I am beginning to understand what the ascendancy classes meant when they spoke or, indeed, boasted about old retainers.

'I am your personal tramp,' he informed me in a rare fit of indulgence some time ago, 'and I am here to see that no other tramp annoys you. If you are to be annoyed I am the man who's going to do it. Who has a better right! I am, after all, your tramp. Therefore, thou shalt not have false tramps before you.'

I decided to keep my mouth firmly closed. He is a tramp who uses any and all things I say for his own ends. He can, as the poet said, cite scripture for all his purpose.

There is one great advantage about having one's own personal tramp. Tramps have their own code, a code that is rigidly observed by themselves.

'Never mind what Fentiles think,' he said righteously, 'it is what we, the brotherhood, think that matters.'

No, I didn't mean to say Gentiles. Fentiles is what I said and Fentiles is what I'll stick to. Let me explain about Fentiles. It is the name given by our friend the tramp to all those who are not tramps. It is a corruption of Infantiles. Fentiles, therefore, in his eyes are what you and I are gentle reader. Personally I am extremely grateful since I know this man's capacity for heaping abuse on people and for all his skill at labelling people, labelling them so that the label sticks and cannot be washed away by time or by detergent, often quite unfairly just because the label·would not buy him drinks or listen to his ideas.

The reader may interject here with the suggestion that customers should be protected from this sort of treatment but I would point out that it is not my function to do so unless they are incapacitated and cannot move of their own accord. The customers under attack are free to move away to another area. However let us suppose that our friend pursues them to the second area, which I regard as an area of refuge, then their liberties have been challenged and it is my duty to insist that the gentleman responsible behaves himself.

Generally speaking, customers in public houses are well able to look after themselves. That is why they venture into public houses in the first place. There is always a gamble attached to sojourning in public houses. One is never totally safe regardless of the high standards of the establishments one visits. One blackguard can disrupt the peace and harmony of any given public house and feel free to do so until the law arrives to remove him. We publicans may not ourselves remove blackguards even if we were able.

This again is what attracts law-abiding people to the public house, the element of risk, the prospect of being abused, castigated, interfered with or assaulted. Some customers go so far as to wear public house clothes lest drink be spilled on their Sunday bests. There is the prospect of being savaged, ravaged and contaminated. Few as they are who are left, the last remaining breeds of fleas still prefer public houses to cinemas, theatres and bingo halls.

Let us return to our friend the tramp. There is no such thing as a resident tramp. His very calling militates totally against permanency of tenure. There is one great advantage though in having one's own tramp and it is that all other tramps are discouraged while he is around.

Just as commercial travellers defer gracefully to each other when they meet in shops and other business houses, so does the tramp stop at the entrance when he beholds another tramp in residence. It is all part of the code of the tramp. There is no handbook for the behaviour of tramps. There is no need. Tramps observe their own rules and woe betide the member who breaks it.

I look forward to the temporary return of my own personal tramp now that he is safely elsewhere. I need him from time to time to ward off worse. I also need him to provoke me. One of the great fears of all writers and this one in particular is the awful prospect of becoming sedentary. My personal tramp is sometimes so annoying that he occasionally sets me fuming and, therefore, on my toes. A fuming writer will take on anything but a sedentary writer is a danger to himself and others. By others I mean those who are likely to be bored by him.

Provocation is to me what the raindrop is to the parched flower, what the scalding droplet is to the unfortunate cat.

We were arguing one night about pishogues and the evil effects they are likely to have upon innocent people. The subject of magpies came up. You know the rhyme: one for sorrow, two for joy, three to get married, four to die, five for silver, six for gold and seven for a story that was never told. My friend the tramp had been listening respectfully up to this. Then he put in his spoke.

'A magpie,' said he, 'has no more to do with bad luck than a meat pie.'

This audacious comment succeeded in infuriating the scholarly gentleman who had been holding forth for over thirty-five uncontradicted years on the subject of magpies and pishogues. Blows were avoided when the tramp made his way under the scholar's legs and out the door.

One night as we stood talking in the street the rain came down, sparing nobody. An important man from the business sector of the town was hurrying by when our friend forestalled him.

'Quick,' said the tramp, 'go after April and tell her she forgot her rain.' Give the businessman his due he seemed to enjoy this allusive direction.

'So she's gone off without it again,' he said as he stroked his chin. He looked up and down the street and shook his head.

'Too late,' he said, 'she's gone.'

I wonder when this personal tramp of mine will show up again. He disappeared last year for the entire summer. Then my wife and I spotted him in Galway. He was a different man. When we hailed him he was conscious and nervous. I had the awful feeling for a moment that he had sold out and become somebody's tramp. I knew, however, that this was not strictly true.

I discovered the truth the following night after the races. There he was in another pub annoying several customers at the same time. So that was it. I was his by winter and another publican's by summer. I decided not to interfere. My wife and I left quickly lest he spot us. He was dressed as usual, a peaked cap, a shabby raincoat and a high class umbrella hanging from his arm. Could that man carry an umbrella! He carried it as though it had never been stolen, as though he had been born with an umbrella on his arm.

Visitations

This is a time of year for strange visitations. The harvest is almost secure, the apples are ripening and the nuts faintly coppering in sylvan glades. All, so to speak, is being looked after so that those who bear burdens may now unload them, however temporarily, and fare forth in search of harmless diversion.

There's no year around this time that I am not visited by an unusual male with unusual tales to tell. This is not to say that females are not unusual. No indeed for there is nothing as unusual as a female regardless of age.

This year's visitor arrived at 7.30 wearing a bright silk scarf, sports jacket and pants, wearing a white shirt and white slippers and, most important, wearing his sixty odd years as though they were a sweet two and twenty. He was an engaging chap sure enough with a light but never shallow line of patter. He refused to disclose either his name or his county.

'Obscurity,' said he, as he quaffed a chilled lager, 'is the best of bodyguards and as for counties,' he continued, 'you know what a county is?'

'Tell me,' I entreated.

'A county,' said he smoothly, 'is an organisation that revels in its own imagined supremacy.'

'And often tells cheap jokes about its neighbours,' I suggested by way of rounding off his observation. He shook my hand.

'Well put,' he said and found himself a high stool. He did not have to tell me he was a bachelor. I could tell that he was nothing else but I guessed that he would have a spinster sister for he did not look run-down as some uncared-for bachelors do.

'How's your sister?' I asked, sussing him out as far as I dare.

'I have no sister,' said he rather plaintively, 'only a mother but she's hale and hearty thank God.'

'Girlfriend?' I asked.

'Not right now,' he replied. 'I believe in promiscuity and that seems to have gone out of fashion. Anyway,' he continued blithely, 'life without promiscuity is like Irish stew without mutton.'

I didn't agree of course but I had to concede that he had a way of putting things.

Just then some young ladies entered. He exited via the toilet door and emerged almost immediately, comb-ed, washed and smoothed. Never before had I beheld a man so susceptible to the flutterings of ladies' eyelids. He insisted on paying for their drinks and entertained them for a while with some trivial anecdotes. When he offered them a lift to Ballybunion they made it clear that while he was attractive and manly and decent he was also too advanced in years for young damsels in their twenties. He took it all well and I asked him if he had any notion of settling down.

'No,' said he, 'Mother wouldn't approve. I take what I can although my latest attempt at seduction was rebuffed.'

'Oh!' I said.

'Oh indeed!' said he, and he went on to tell us that she was a widow who lived on the same avenue as he. Apparently he dug her garden, re-built her turf-shed, lopped her branches but left not a single dent on her chastity.

'She would have me all right on a permanent basis,' he confided, 'but Mother wouldn't approve.'

The girls told him that he should ignore his mother and suit himself.

'If you knew my mother,' said he, 'you wouldn't say that.'

The girls departed and we were left alone. I came to the conclusion that his mother was not as bad as he painted her, that he was the author of his own bachelorhood. He must have read my thoughts for his attitude took a turn for the worse. A cloud crossed his wrinkle-free features. He rose, swallowed his drink, ignored the change from his ten pound note which lay on the counter and then, with the emphasised indifference of the true snob, cleared his throat, bade me good evening and was gone.

I'll probably have to wait until next year before I meet anybody so colourful again.

Overhearing

The best way to enjoy oneself free of charge is to listen to one's fellow human beings, listen carefully that is. They have important things to say and they have funny things to say but unless we give them our undivided attention we will miss much. Yesterday in the bar I was being interviewed by a man from American television about the great matchmaker Dan Paddy Andy and about made marriages. The pub was full of customers at the time and most listened avidly out of politeness. One gentleman, however, that is if the expression on his face was anything to go by, did not seem to approve of my observations and during a lull in shooting he addressed himself to his female companion. 'Arranged marriages,' said he, 'remind me of ballot papers with only one candidate.'

I complimented him and he was astonished and he was astounded. He could not believe that I had overheard so I explained to him that overhearing rather than eavesdropping was one of my strong points. Later that night I was talking about night-time to the visitor. There were several others on the premises and when I pointed out to my listener that the night was for cats, bats and lovers some tittered while others smiled anaemically which was their way of saying that they had heard it all before.

'The night is for snots,' said a fat man who sat on his own in a corner. He spoke half to himself and half to the world in a tone which suggested that he couldn't care less whether any chance listeners agreed with him or not.

'Well said,' I called out to him. He blushed modestly and repaid my praise with the following:

At dead of night when darkness enfolds the scene,
At dead of night when snots mature unseen.

If I had not overheard I would never have been presented with the unique couplet which, incidentally, I had never heard before. It was the assiduous way in which I kept my ears cocked that paid such dividends.

While I like listening to humans there are others who like to listen to other creatures, notably birds and I must confess that I am greatly addicted to birdsong myself and to the soft, romantic wailing of cats. So too do I like the crying of curlews in the rain and the mewing of seabirds on lonely coastlines.

I like also the yowling of dogs in the dead of night but I must say this about my neighbourhood dogs in all fairness. Oh ye hypocritical dogs of Listowel who howl sanctimoniously with the Angelus bell and then go soil the streets as if it were a divine right! Listowel's a beautiful town but we have more dog droppings than are strictly necessary.

I must say here that we cannot lay the blame on the owners all the time. Some dogs are natural defecators like their human counterparts. In the bar the conversation turned to humans again or more precisely to humans who tell jokes and a number had been tossed around by a few young men who had presented themselves for alcohol at the bar counter.

The language in which they dressed their contributions was uncouth and I was on the point of reminding them that we were not prepared to put up with such talk when my task was made easy by a good-looking woman of mature years who yawned and in yawning managed to accompany with a long, loud sigh.

'She's yawning,' said one of the youths although it was none of his business.

Said her ladyship, stifling a second contribution: 'I became so impregnated by your tasteless jokes that I had to give birth to something and I think the yawn was the most appropriate.'

It had the desired effect and the visitors greatly modified their language thereafter.

Watching Diners

One of the better-known pastimes of my boyhood was watching people eating. In those days there were no sliced pans and very often great feats of grinding were necessary especially where the slices, cut by hand, were thicker than usual. Remember too that false teeth were still a luxury and the average male, especially from the poorer sections of the community, was rarely possessed of the teeth he started out with. He would be lucky to have half or even less.

Watching a man with poorly-deployed teeth chewing crusts was as intriguing and entertaining as watching an aged lion eating donkey-meat in the menageries of the many circuses which came to town in those days. The facial grimaces involved were enough to frighten the life out of the unwary onlooker who stumbled upon the mastication process by accident. Also there were grunts and groans so great was the physical and mental effort involved.

Our favourite vantage point was outside the large glass window of a pie shop at the bottom of the street and our favourite subject was a fat man who ate his pie with one hand while he kept his face covered with the other. Like the ostrich he believed that nobody could see him if he kept his hand over his face. He was a shy sort and always managed to find a place as far away from the window as possible. Other times he would face into a corner and look furtively around him between mouthfuls as though he had no right to be there. He had no teeth that could be seen but they were there all right at the sides of his mouth, about four or five in number. Because of this he would be obliged to move the food to either the left or the right side of the mouth. The result was that much of his pie wound up on the table where he unfailingly recovered it when he had finished the plate. He lapped it up as though it were an aftercourse.

I once saw him eating sausages. He put them into his mouth sideways and broke them out with the side teeth. Then he returned them to the centre of the mouth where he savoured them fully before swallowing.

There was another with false teeth. The bother was that he used to take them out while he was eating. So ignorant were we garsúns at the time that we would press our curious faces to the glass the better to study his facial antics as he strove manfully to chew his food aided by nothing more than his naked gums. In those days there was quite a lot of fat meat in the mutton pies which were the standard fare in most of the restaurants in the town. Fat was supposed to be good for a person in those benighted times.

'Look at the Eskimos,' my mother used to say. 'Look at how fat they are and all they eat is blubber.'

'And candles,' my father would add in his helpful way although he would never say it again after a younger sister swallowed half a candle, a mission candle at that which had been specially blessed for the renouncing of the devil.

'Eat your fat or you'll fall away to nothing,' was a common admonishment by neighbouring mothers.

'Wouldn't they love to have that now in China,' they would say. At the time there was nearly always a famine in some part of China. The communist countries might not be much use at granting civil liberties but I'll say one thing for them. They knew how to starve people.

In Ballybunion the main front window of the then Castle Hotel was a great spot from which to view the diners. We would press our faces to the window and pretend we were starving but it didn't have the slightest effect on the diners. They were far more sophisticated than the men who dined at the pie shop down our street. They tucked napkins under their chins and sat straight upon their chairs. The only weapon the pie-man had was a spoon but these had knives and forks, dessert and soup spoons and fish-knives. How many innocent Irishmen were baffled by fish-knives! For years I tried in vain to cut fish with a fish-knife but I had to give it up and return to the normal knife. My Uncle Jack was right. 'There's something fishy about those danged fish-knives,' he used always say.

The only use I could ever find for fish-knives as a garsún was for pinking peas across the dining-room whenever we paid a rare visit to a hotel dining-room. I tried mashed potatoes once but caught a priest accidentally on the face with a spatter that temporarily blinded him. My father nearly murdered me on that occasion. It was no doubt a sacrilege.

We were guilty of causing great discomfiture to innocent country people in the pie shops of the period. Three or four of us would select the most harmless looking type in the dining area and stare at him remorselessly as he spooned his pie and soup to his mouth. What common blackguards we were and how we glared at him whenever he looked apprehensively in our direction! There was a mixture of fear and guilt on his face as he ground his food in the chamber of his mouth. The soup would dribble down the sides of his chin whenever he opened his mouth to rebuke us. He, poor fellow, was being troubled by his conscience believing that we were homeless urchins on the brink of dying from starvation.

There was another chap of advanced years who used to pull his overcoat over his head to shut out nosy onlookers. This man was the noisiest feeder we ever came across. He reminded me of Moran's dog farther up the street. Moran's dog didn't really eat. He slobbered and sometimes he moaned as if the chore of sustaining himself with food was altogether too much for him.

The man who pulled the coat over his head used also sigh and moan and even grunt while he downed his mutton pie. I remember well that he used to be totally exhausted when his repast was finished. He was hardly able to wipe his mouth with the sleeve of his coat. I'll say one thing for him. There was no grandeur about him. He always blew his nose into his palm and rubbed it to his trousers seat and he never used anything but his coat sleeve to clean his face.

I still wonder why one of our victims didn't rush

out of the shop and implant a boot on our backsides. They would have been entitled to do so. Sometimes the woman who owned the shop would send out the girl who assisted her and she would shoo us off swinging a wet dishcloth.

Those were the days. Everybody has false teeth now or, at least those who haven't, have their natural teeth. Signs on people do not grind their food anymore and fat or gristle are now regarded as deadly enemies. How things have changed! Now they say 'eat that fat at your peril', whereas when we were garsúns they would say 'get that fat inside o' you and you'll pulverise Joe Louis'.

Invalids

This world is full of people who look worse than they are. A number of my relatives go around like invalids all the time because they haven't the gall to go around looking healthy. Our family, and yours too, I'm sure, has always been afflicted with its fair share of professional convalescents. In fact if things were to change I don't know what I'd do without the whining and the complaining and the long faces and the shuffling and the shifting.

I don't think I'd be able to carry on I've become so used to it and there's the dreadful thought that if the ailments were to go away altogether they would surely be replaced by something worse because there's a fly in every ointment and when one fly goes there's another ready to take his place.

I have one particular connection who can be very trying but there may be worse waiting to take his place. He is not a relation. He is a distant in-law but distant as he is he has the same potential as distant thunder clouds, distant rainstorms and distant explosions. He would arrive at any minute. He paid me one of his rare visits last week. It beats me how he always manages to look so pale. He is a martyr, according to himself, to many unknown and incurable diseases and there is no moment of the day or night that he does not endure some form of suffering.

A relation told me lately that the reason he is so

pale is that he avoids the sun the way a lazy man avoids work. The sun is anathema to him for the good reason that if he were to expose himself to it there would be the danger of his face assuming a healthy hue.

'You will always find him,' said the relation, 'at the shady side of the house when the sun is about its business.'

When he arrived on the premises he stood at the doorway for a while wheezing and whining and nattering and snuffling and casting baleful looks all around.

'God help us,' said a visitor, 'that poor chap isn't long for the world.'

I recalled about forty years before that an uncle of mine passed the very same remark about the very same man. The uncle is dead and the very same man is to the good.

All eyes were upon him as he stood near the door. Then an elderly woman, struck by compassion, raised herself with considerable difficulty and found him a seat. She asked him if he was all right but do you think he favoured her with an answer after her kindness to him. He sat for a moment and indicated by a series of the most terrifying facial grimaces that his buttocks found the seat unbearable. He rose with the customary wheezing and dragged his feet after him as though they were somebody else's.

Slowly he made his way to the bar counter and fixed his eyes on me as though I was personally to blame for all his imagined woes. I was having none of it.

'You're looking well!' I called out to him. This stopped him in his tracks. The enormity of such a statement was tantamount to blasphemy but before he could utter a word I told him that I had never seen him looking better. The cold truth was that he had a hollow look about him like a sausage roll without the sausage.

'Give me a half o' brandy,' he said. I duly dispensed the brandy and when he had it paid for he demanded a drop of port.

'Sandeman's,' he insisted. This is an old trick. He knew well that if he called for a brandy and port together he would be charged for the port whereas only a heartless publican, or so he gave the impression, would charge a poor invalid with a foot in the grave for a drop of port.

I am happy to be able to report that he didn't die on that occasion and I have the eeriest of feelings that he will be calling after we have all gone.

Corner Boy or Bystander

The letter which lies opened before me could be said to be the observation of a reasonable man. He nevertheless accuses me, and who's to say that he's not right, of being sympathetic to corner boys and prejudiced against innocent bystanders.

'You glorify corner boys,' he states, 'who do nothing except draw the dole and rub their backsides against corners all day. But let an innocent bystander be struck down and you're all for kicking him. The innocent bystander has as much right to stand and look around him as the corner boy has to lean against the corner.'

There is a good deal more but obscenity rears its rude head and it's time to stop quoting. He makes a good point however does 'Straw Boy' as he signs himself under his real name.

Firstly let me say that not all corner boys draw the dole. Large numbers of corner boys work for a living and spend only their recreation hours at corners. Some forego meals and drinks and even marriage so that they can devote their lives to their corners. They must never be compared with innocent bystanders described by another reader as follows: 'They are,' he writes, 'perverts of the worst kind and if I had my way I would shoot one in every four. I caught one recently admiring himself free of charge in a mirror which occupies the centre of my shop window. No one else would look in the mirror while he stood there. Two nice-looking girls stopped to rearrange their hair. They're always stopping there and they are welcome. Ladies have been stopping at my window for years to avail of the mirror. Ask anyone in town and they'll tell you the same. Finally I had to take him by the scruff of the neck and move him along. He threatened me with the law. He was a professor of something or other but it wasn't manners. Threatening me with law imagine, and the mirror my own!'

I fully sympathise with the shop-owner in question and he is to be complimented for his attitude towards members of the opposite sex. I'm not surprised to learn that the innocent bystander in this instance was a professor. It is a known fact that academics, more than any other profession, are committed to innocent bystanding. Next in line come researchers and scientists. These are closely followed by handymen who never miss an opportunity to dawdle on their way to work. Not all handymen are innocent bystanders. I say this for my own protection for I am dependent on handymen from time to time but it is true to say that they make up a significant percentage of innocent bystanders.

To my mind and, of course, this is purely a personal opinion, the worst and most heedless of all the varieties of innocent bystanders who torment and intimidate other human beings is your gangly individual with a take-away box or quite simply a carton of chips in his hand.

This individual cannot and will not eat his chips or

whatever with his back to a wall or in a shop doorway like civilised people. No! He must first locate the scene of a row or argument or altercation. When he finds one to his liking, and the bloodier the better, he ends his search. Then and not till then does he commence with the business of eating. He will never look at his fare. He will do everything from locating the chip or sausage or chicken chunk to conveying it to the open mouth without ever taking his eyes from the violent activities in front of him. Munching like a pony he follows the action with an unholy stare. So curious does he become that he gets carried away altogether and places himself too close to the battleground. The inevitable happens and he is struck with a clenched fist. There is no malice. He just simply happened to be in the way.

Your frustrated pugilist very often strikes at a so-called innocent bystander just to get him out of the way so that he can get at the real enemy. Who is to blame him if, after finding an easy target, he forgets the real enemy and goes all out for the innocent bystander who generally cannot and will not hit back! The frustrated pugilist may amuse himself no end and indulge in some exceedingly stylish boxing safe in the knowledge that there will be no retaliation.

Can you imagine the unmitigated gall of the injured bystander who complains of the assault to the police when he knows full well that he is the author of his own misfortune. How low can people stoop! How malicious can they get!

In the bar the other night an elderly gentleman came up with a rather bizarre idea.

'I have suffered my share,' said he, 'at the hands of innocent bystanders. One afternoon in the main street an old lady collapsed in front of my eyes. I went to the poor creature's aid immediately. While I was endeavouring heroically to lift her to her feet an innocent bystander came along and assumed the role of observer. He had in his hand a packet of goldgrain biscuits. While he observed my hectic efforts he munched furiously, transferring biscuits from the package to his mouth at top speed and all the time he never took his eyes off myself or the old lady.

'He made no attempt whatsoever to help me. I asked him to come to my aid but a sly smile spread across his face and then suddenly he turned. His attention had been captured by a dogfight and I was left to the unequal struggle on my own.'

So ends the elderly gentleman's story. It was then that he put forward his idea.

'I would be in favour,' said he, 'of forming a special task force who would round up innocent bystanders and have them removed to special detention centres or camps where they might be trained to behave in the same fashion as responsible human beings.'

Another imbiber who had also been the victim of an innocent bystander outrage came to the fore.

'Is there a danger,' said he, 'that the innocent bystander might be confused with the innocent corner boy?'

'Never!' we all retorted at once, our tones filled with outrage. I was at pains to explain that the corner boy never deserts his corner except to go home to bed or his meals. He may shift from one side of the corner to the other or may he stand tiptoe the better to view a distant fracas but he will get in nobody's way while so doing.

More importantly it is widely known that corner boys and innocent bystanders are exact opposites. The moment an innocent bystander arrives at a corner occupied by a mature corner boy he is immediately dispatched elsewhere without ceremony. For this we must be eternally grateful to all corner boys. Without them you would have a glut of innocent bystanders blocking our streets and choking our thoroughfares. The corner boy knows a pest when he sees one. He can always be depended upon to take the appropriate action. If you should seek a temporary refuge from the prying eyes of innocent bystanders you would be well advised to seek sanctuary at a well-named corner.

Salute Ye One Another

At a wedding recently I was taken to task by a pleasant young female because of a piece I wrote many moons ago which dealt with saluting people. Now I have written about saluting on several occasions but it is the opinion of the young lady in question that I should discourage people from saluting other people. Her reasons are valid enough. She says that people who drive cars are endangering other people's lives when they salute other drivers. She also maintained that pedestrians should concentrate upon their own comings and goings rather than salute acquaintances and friends not to mention run-of-the-mill passers-by. I did not argue the toss with the girl at the time but I promised her that I would deal with the subject, for the final time, when the mood caught me.

Not saluting people will, I believe, ultimately do far more harm than good. For instance let us suppose you are driving along any given roadway and an acquaintance salutes you with a wave of the hand from the driving seat of another car which happens to be travelling in the opposite direction. If you deliberately refuse to return the salute you could be the cause of affecting the unsaluted party's concentration and thus contribute to a crash or even loss of life.

What this young lady does not seem to know is that the people of this world, regardless of their stations or ages, are in constant need of reassurance.

With no one to reassure them there are many people who would just disintegrate or become anti-social. In the absence of a system, state-sponsored or otherwise, whereby people would be reassured regularly we are left with the simple salute. It is, in my humble opinion, the only inexpensive means of reassuring neglected pedestrians and motorists that there is somebody out there who cares. I'm out there for instance. I feel that everybody must be saluted without reason. Obviously if you are in a dangerous quarter of a large city where crime is rampant you would be well advised, especially if you are a female, to suspend your saluting activities until you return to safer climes, better still, climes where you are known.

Saluting strange men in dangerous surroundings is akin to a deer saluting a cheetah or a lamb saluting a lion. Imagine a rabbit out for an innocent stroll suddenly pausing and addressing a nod or a wave of a forepaw to a hungry fox. Beware then where you salute!

Reassurance like commonsense is one of the world's rarer commodities. If there was enough reassurance to go around there would be no despondency or depression but then, says the gentle reader, what would happen to depression-treaters and despondency-treaters and what would happen to the employees of chemical concerns who manufacture pills and potions for the lifting of depression? This is the problem about providing solutions for the pressing problems. The birth of a solution means the birth of another problem.

However let us press on. Some people go to extraordinary lengths not to salute other people. I have seen
them in action. It has even happened to myself. A man
who owes me a few quid which I don't require always
covers his face with his umbrella when we pass by. If
he hasn't an umbrella he disappears into shops or up
alleyways.

Then there are what I call natural slighters who set
up innocent acquaintances and even neighbours for a
cheery salute and then, at the last minute when the
other party has committed itself to a salute, the setter-
upper doesn't salute at all. This has the same effect on
the unsaluted party as a thwarted sneeze.

Then there are those who will not return salutes
for the simple reason that they have been unsaluted
by the saluter in the past. Then there is jealousy. I
knew a woman in our street who cocked her snoot in
the air at all those who she believed were better off
than she was. Take it from me my friends you are
better off saluting regardless of the provocation to
which you feel you have been subjected over the years.
Not saluting precipitates chain reaction. If you fail to
return the salute of an acquaintance then the sons
and daughters of that acquaintance may end up not
saluting you or yours. The end result of all this could
lead to nobody saluting, nobody doffing or waving or
winking or yoo-hooing. You want this to happen? If
you do, then don't salute people!

Believe me when I say that a large percentage of
the world's population is starved for the want of a salute. When I was a small boy there was a man in town

who used to give us youngsters a half-penny to salute him when there were people around on occasions such as race days or after foot-ball games or coming from Mass. He would give us the half-penny with the instruction that we were to say 'Hello Mister Moogle. How are you Mister Moogle'.

Of course his name wasn't Moogle. I can't disclose his real name because his descendants are still in the neighbourhood and if they become aware that I mentioned their ancestor's hunger for salutations they might never salute me again. This happens all the time. The tragedy is that while I would know why I am not being saluted the vast majority who go unsaluted do not know the reason why. This can be very frustrating and they resolve there and then not to salute 'that so and so' as they call the non-saluter, ever again. I am certain that there are many people who simply pine away for want of a salute. Remember this when you feel like cocking your snoot in the air. You may unwittingly be bringing about the downfall of another or is this what you have in mind in the first place? If so you are being grossly unchristian and will one day be called aside and asked to explain yourself by you know who.

Of course it must also be said that there are large numbers of people suffering from delusions of grandeur which I have always regarded as one of the worst maladies known to medical science.

We had a lady in our street once and she would salute nobody. My father, God be good to him, would say that she was right 'for,' he would ask in his homely way, especially if he had a few jars taken, 'who the hell is anybody anyway?'

Then there are unfortunate folk who suffer from surfeits of rebuffs over the years and will not risk saluting horses and even donkeys. I have seen sane men salute cows and bullocks in secluded places. I daresay some of them do it to keep their hands in.

In conclusion I would advise the gentle reader to salute wherever possible even if no encouragement is provided by the party about to be saluted. Better still we might cleave to the dictum of the ancient maxim: Salute ye one another in the highways and the by-ways, at the going up of the moon and the going down of the sun. Amen.

Take Your Time

I have grown sick and tired of reading day in, day out, about how to improve one's sexual performance as if nothing else mattered. Yet in spite of this ongoing bombardment by so-called experts there has been no detectable, over-all improvement. Billions have been spent in the pursuit of the elusive cure for sexual deterioration and yet there have been no dramatic results.

One wonders if it's all a vast conspiracy organised and funded by the chemical companies. There are men and women out there in need of succour, failures in the copulatory stakes as it were and while they languish millions are spent every day on questionable treatment.

Here now are some findings which were arrived at in these here licensed premises only last Thursday. The usual patrons were gathered, the fortunes of some greatly bolstered by the state which pays out modest sums to the unemployed, the disabled, the deserted, the widowed and many other deserving cases on that particular day.

The first contribution came from a widow with a local base and a reputation for common sense.

'What I always found,' she said, 'was that if you want them to operate you must keep them cool.'

'Keep them cool?' asked a Ballylongford farmer who happened to be in town to back a horse.

'The men,' the widow answered. 'Don't let them fuss themselves or be agitated and don't give them bad news or they'll fall down on the job entirely. Give 'em plenty to eat and drink and don't rush 'em.'

She obviously spoke from experience and was supported in her opinions by a second widow.

'If the men,' said she, 'had less talk they'd do better. All talk will get them nowhere. The man that don't talk much is always the best for what is now called sex. We usen't call it by that name at all.'

'And what used ye call it?' a Ballybunion man asked. The man in question had an extensive vocabulary in this respect and was simply soliciting an extension to his collection. The widow came to his aid.

'It used be called "the other thing" when I was growing up. You see people were a way more polite in them days and you'd never catch them using a vulgar word. Personally I never heard the word sex until I was forty or so.'

'The "other thing"!' the Ballylongford farmer echoed the phrase thoughtfully. 'I like it,' he said, 'it's not vulgar and children wouldn't understand it.'

There was silence for a while, a longer than usual silence which I suspect was caused by the delicate nature of the subject under discussion. North Kerry folk are sensitive and articulate and are always careful to express themselves in inoffensive language.

'What I was told was this,' said a farmer from Moyvane who had come to town for bird seed. 'You should always leave off work before you get tired. Don't you see the clever man rising from the table, how he leaves a good bit on the plate so as to keep the fat away and keep himself trim. 'Tis the same with the "other thing". If you over work you'll be fit for nothing after.'

'I couldn't agree more,' said the Ballybunion man, 'and I'll tell ye one thing for sure and that is that too much singing is no good either. I seen men singing themselves hoarse while it was the man that hadn't a note went off with the woman.'

'Certainly,' said the widow who had spoken first, 'too much of anything is bad. A man must moderate himself or he'll be wore out.'

'If a man don't spare himself,' said the second widow, 'he'll sleep the minute he hits the pillows.'

'Take the strain off the man,' said the first widow, 'and he won't let you down.'

'You must take into account too,' said the second widow, 'that an idle man is fit for anything. A worried man won't raise a gallop and a rich man has other things on his mind but an idle man with no money has nothing else but the "other thing".'

'The hardworking man has no chance then?' suggested an overworked labourer who chanced to be passing through with his spouse.

'I didn't say that,' said the second widow. 'What I said was that the rich and the hardworking have too many other things on their mind.'

'I heard,' said the Ballylongford farmer, 'that trapped wind was a great deterrent, that it hampered a man no end in his sexual endeavours.'

'Anything that is trapped,' the first widow responded, 'inside the body will cause pain and damage and I can well believe that trapped wind will do a man no good in the business of what we're talking about.'

'What about undescended testicles?' asked the Ballybunion man.

'Well now,' said the first widow as she drained the last drop of vodka and tonic from her glass, 'I know nothing about them.'

'What goes up must come down,' said the second widow. The conversation went on and on but the males were now less forthcoming in their contributions, no doubt aware of the fact that too much talk might well militate against future performances. They weren't exactly tongue-tied. Rather were they more economical and as a result the standard of comment was raised.

'It's not the things you do or take,' said the first widow. 'It's the thing you shouldn't do and shouldn't take.'

'What shouldn't one take?' asked a local drunkard, one of many who calls on Thursdays to see if anything is doing.

'One shouldn't take too much booze,' came the ready answer, 'and one shouldn't take too much exercise. One shouldn't take too much fat or too many sweet things. Remember a little goes a long way and you won't go far wrong.'

'To be in a hurry too is not good,' the second widow nodded her head solemnly.

'Tight shoes are no good either,' said the first widow.

'Nor is tight collars,' said the second.

So we see gentle reader that it's not what we take

but what we don't take.

'Above all,' said both widows in unison, 'take your time.'

The Hots

Fooling around with words can be a dangerous business. It can't be avoided however if one is in the writing business. When I was younger I used to believe that there were too many words in the world and then when I would find myself under pressure from an editor I would come to the conclusion that there weren't enough.

Often I would be obliged to institute a search for the right word just as a mason might look for a suitable stone with which to carry on with the building of a wall. I would sometimes be forced to use two words instead of one. I know now that there are certain commodities, instances and occasions for which there are no single words, for which special words have to be freshly minted.

There will be readers who may say that I have an awful neck inciting people to make up new words when old words are not immediately available. My dear friends let me remind you that there is no law which forbids the coining of new words no more than there is a law forbidding the coining of new phrases or new sentences. If there was such a law there wouldn't be any readable books or entertaining plays. We have, therefore, every right to create new words when the need arises. Necessity is the mother of invention as the man said when he made false teeth from timber. When we cannot make do with what we have we must become inventive.

There is a gentleman who frequently visits these here premises with his wife, a man who does not wish his business to be disclosed to curious onlookers. Public houses are great places for curious onlookers possessed of extraordinary hearing. Not only are they not satisfied with their own drinks but they find the night tedious unless they are fully informed about the drinking habits of others. This information is available only if one is prepared to look and listen with maximum concentration. With constant practice it is possible to deduce what the couple at the other end of the bar are having and also the quantities involved.

Consequently the gentleman who does not wish his business to be known must perforce create words that will baffle the most alert listener.

When he asked me to dispense a lopener and a Friesian I did so without the slightest difficulty. A Friesian as everybody knows is simply a Black and White which is a well-known brand of Scotch whereas a lopener is a vodka and tonic. The reason I have no problem filling his order is because I have been doing so for years and I am familiar with his lingo.

A lopener, if the gentle reader will forgive me, is short for a leg opener. Sometimes he might call for a large leg opener by simply saying 'and a doublopener for the missus'.

This happens as the reader may well have deduced after rows when the couple are hell bent on making up and eventually cleaving unto each other.

You must agree that it would never do if the curious listener became privy to such choice knowledge about his neighbours or acquaintances. Therefore there is a special need for new words on such occasions.

I remember too how my mother used to be extremely circumspect when visiting the butcher. Nearly always there would be a resident gossipmonger or two in the vicinity of the counter so that women were often so embarrassed that they withdrew until these interlopers might have departed. My mother was well prepared for such contingencies.

'Himself was allaphonting last night,' she would say to the butcher, to which he would reply, 'Ah, God help us all'.

Then he would discreetly, with his broad back covering his operations, prepare the appropriate meat which was nearly always boiling lamb or mutton. My father had great faith in such fare and the soup there from whenever he had a sick head. What allaphonting meant was that my father had been drinking late at Alla Sheehy's pub the night before.

The pub in question was next door but one to our home in Church Street and it could be truthfully stated that all the Keanes were blooded there, beerwise. Although allaphonting may sound like gallivanting and indeed it might well be rhymed with gallivanting it has little relation to the word in question.

To gallivant according to all major dictionaries is to go about seeking pleasure and diversion. My mother often applied the word to my young sisters when they would arrive home breathless and late for meals.

To allaphont was, in short, to sit at the phont of Alla or font of Alla, there to slake one's thirst legitimately and to pay for it with coin of the realm or lacking same to drink on the nail and to repay the monies due when one's ship came in as the saying goes. In my heyday I was a great allaphonter and have nothing but the happiest and most cheerful memories of times well spent in that incomparable hostelry.

Then there was Curlyitis which simply meant that we had spent a while at Curly O'Connor's, another approved hostelry further down the street. It was in Curly's in fact that we invented the character Tom Doodle whose joyful antics took the rancour and bitterness out of local politics. This happy state still exists in the town of Listowel due in no small measure to the birth of Tom and, of course, to the good sense of the townspeople.

There is too an irreplaceable word which was born in America some years ago and which I greatly admire being something of a word lover among other things. The word, of course, is Hots. It was introduced into our house by an American relative who came to spend a holiday with us many years ago and who, may I say in passing, frequently enjoyed allaphonting and was often subject to Curlyitis.

He used the word when it came to his attention that a brother of mine had become temporarily infatuated with a young lady up the street who was not, as far as we knew, even aware of the existence of my brother.

'Ah!' said the Yank. 'So he's got the hots for this

dame.'

We were all greatly taken with the word and it must be said that it has no comparable word in our speech. The hots was not strictly love and it didn't sound very romantic so what was it then?

It was, I believe, a cross between infatuation and lust and could not, therefore, be expected to last. It is a disease to which we have all been subject at one time or another and it always passes, praise be to God.

Words

When I was much younger than I am now, less grey,
less prone to the pains of age and infinitely more
mobile physically and mentally there, used to be a
grown man who hung upon my every word. He is now
gone from the scene, gone to that bourne from which,
as the poet says, no traveller ever returns.

I don't know from where he originally came. Rum-
our had it that he was reared in an orphanage. Anyway he wound up working with a farmer in this local-
ity. The reason he hung upon my every word was that
he had very few of his own. How shall I put it? Let me
say that he had enough to be going on with but none
at all to spare or none which might be contributed to a
conversation out of, or above, the norm. We became
fast friends. He used to follow our football team to
most of the games and he was among our most
staunch supporters.

'There will no one blackguard ye,' he used to say,
'while I'm knocking around.' The reason he hung upon
my every word was that he loved big words and, of all
our company, I was the one who used big words the
most. I didn't always use them in the proper context,
at least not for starters, but with the passage of time I
began to understand the ways of big words and was
better able to deal with them. I discovered, not before
too long thank God, that one was generally better off
without them. After I made my discovery I rarely used

a big word, settling for smaller ones and only using the larger when it became an absolute necessity.

There we'd be, the majority of the football team, in a pub after a game nursing our pints because money was scarce and therefore every mouthful was savoured all the more. Such a climate begets a true appreciation of porter which can last a lifetime and is the first step against excesses. We shall call the man who hung on my every word Wally.

After the second pint our tongues would automatically loosen so that the words ran freely. Wally had little to say. He would listen, hoping to hear a new word, a long one full of resounding vowels and corresponding consonants.

Suddenly he would hear a word he liked. At once would he ensnare it, nurture it by repeating it over and over again and hold it ready for an outing or an occasion which would suit him and suit the word. One of the first words he picked up was salubrious. He ensnared it easily and committed it to memory. I remember I described the pint which I had been drinking as salubrious. I knew at once he had gone for it. His mouth opened and he repeated it silently. For the next several weeks he would use it regularly. Everything became salubrious, the weather when it brightened and held its breath, the full moon and even a referee who had suffered severe criticism from our captain.

'Ah wisha,' said Wally, 'he's a salubrious poor oul' devil all the same.'

He described a High Mass which he had attended as highly salubrious. Then all of a sudden there was no more salubrious. He transferred his affections to perfidious. Everything that did not meet with his approval became perfidious. Even the team we had trounced the previous Sunday was perfidious. What harm but they were as decent a bunch as you could meet. Then one evening while we were training I described an awkward fostook of a fellow who had tripped me as an unconformable nitwit. Nitwit Wally knew but unconformable! now there was a mouthful. It lasted a long time. After several months he eventually got rid of it. Then and not till then did I take the bull by the horns.

'How is it,' I said, 'that we never hear the word salubrious now or perfidious or unconformable. Look at all the words you'd have now if you held on to them.' I didn't tell him he reminded me of a young fellow who had been presented with a new pair of shoes. If unsupervised the youngster would wear them every day until they were completely worn out and only fit for the rubbish dump.

'Words is different,' he said, as though he had read my thoughts. 'Words don't cost anything and there's plenty of 'em there.'

Often in the conveyance of words he would make errors. Transportation of any kind always results in its fair share of accidents, even tragedies. There is always a risk involved especially if there is a heavy load or if the driver is not familiar with a shifty cargo. It is the same with words and Wally was inclined to make more than his fair share of errors.

For instance there was Beechinor's pills. He meant

Beecham's pills of course but there was a pub cum grocery up the street called Beechinor's and it was no bother to Wally to confuse the two.

Then there was Castrated Oil. What was required was Castor Oil but being a farmer's boy Wally would have been familiar with the word castration because of the common or garden demasculation of bull calves and banbhs. The poor creatures have no redress in a world where only man seems to matter.

The word which Wally cherished most was obstreperous. He held on to it far longer than any other. At football games he would turn round and address himself to the supporters of the opposing team and ask them not to be obstreperous.

'What is he?' they would ask. 'Is he a teacher or what?' It was a word which reporters might use to describe a particular set of supporters but it was not a word hostile sets of supporters would use to describe each other.

Other words which were distorted during transportation were asternomical, absoblutely and pernounciation to mention but a few.

Another word of Wally's which caused a good deal of concern and confusion was macerbation. Often during a football game when little would divide the teams he would grow excited. Youngsters among the opposition supporters would know about Wally's weakness. They would goad him into making threats.

'Get out of my sight,' he would shout at them, 'or I'll macerbate the lot of ye.' What he meant of course was macerate but it was so near to the other unmentionable that it provided visiting youths with choice entertainment.

Then there was the club meeting where a player from the club was defending himself against accusations of playing with local teams in other counties. I wasn't at the meeting but Wally was. I had suspected that the player in question would not get much of a hearing for the proof against him was incontrovertible.

'How did he get on?' I asked Wally.

'They amputated him,' said Wally, 'shortly after he stood up to talk.'

Bottomseizure

A woman complained to me on the second night of Listowel Races that she had been sexually harassed on my premises. She wished to know what I was going to do about it. Reluctantly I asked for details and, fair dues to the girl, she spelled them out.

There she had been, standing at the counter with a female friend. She had been standing because no seats were available, 'and this,' said she, 'is where you must carry some of the blame.'

She stoutly maintained that if she had been seated the part of the anatomy which is most frequently subjected to harassment from male sources would not have been at risk. It would have been firmly ensconced on a stool or spread over a seat of lesser altitude. Either way her posterior would have been safe from human hands.

'That's the wretch that did it,' she said and she pointed at a presentable, middle-aged gentleman who stood at a distance sipping delicately from a glass of vodka and bitter lemon.

Realising that he had been singled out he came forward and asked in the most plausible fashion if something was the matter. He seemed to me to be the sort of chap who had no interest whatsoever in female posteriors. In fact if I was asked to testify on his behalf I would have sworn that interfering with female posteriors was the last thought in his head. However, as they say in our native tongue, ní mar síltear bítear. Things are not what they seem.

'I'll tell you what's the matter,' the affronted female wagged a finger at her molester, 'you don't know how to keep your hands to yourself and if I was a man I'd give you a good kick out the door.'

At that moment she lifted her handbag and swung it in the direction of her persecutor. He easily deflected the well-weighted weapon, seized it in his right hand and placed it gently on the counter.

'I plead guilty to laying a hand on your posterior,' he said amicably, 'but I was provoked beyond belief and could not resist the impulse to show my appreciation by fondling it briefly. Let me buy you and your friend a drink in atonement and I swear by my dead mother that I will never lay a hand on your posterior again. I say this,' he concluded, 'knowing that I will have to muster every vestige of my willpower to bypass such an irresistible behind.'

He was a well-spoken scoundrel but he had a way with him and how often in the past has an aggrieved damsel been deceived by the blandishments of a cad! How often has the male deceiver with no more weapons than cajolery and flattery taken the initiative against propriety and honesty not to mention chastity and loyalty and thereby duped the demurest of females and made little of honest men!

It is alas the way of the world and I was not surprised when the friend of the patted party suggested that she let bygones be bygones. The patted party frowned, grinned and then permitted the semblance of a smile to further brighten her already well-illuminated dial.

Thus did she become friends with her natural enemy. He purchased a drink for the pretty pair and for an hour or so regaled them with a collection of genuinely witty tales.

'I see,' I said to the lady who had made the complaint, 'that you have dropped the charges.'

'Yes,' said she, 'he seems a harmless enough type.'

This conclusion, to me at least, seemed to be the very nub of the matter because patters and pinchers of posteriors make no further advances when confronted by their victims. The laying on of the hands, it would seem, is sufficient in itself to satisfy whatever perverse appetite it was that precipitated the covert action in the first place. Later that night there was another outbreak of bottomseizure. This time the male escort of the victim seized the attacker by the throat and would have choked him but for the pleas of the victim. Again the assailant had a soft, gentle face which totally belied his failing which all goes to show that many an innocent man has been slapped in the wrong and that many a guilty party has survived to bottomise another day.

Amateur Critics

Critics on the whole are amiable, well-informed fellows who arrive on time at the theatre and who, mostly under pressure, pen their reviews without prejudice for the papers of the following day. There are exceptions of course. This is true, however, of all callings. In the ranks of the critics are vitriolic sprinklings of verbal thugs and refugees from the literary scene but this is as it should be. They are in a minority and, as the forgiving Kerryman said to his errant offspring, 'there was a blackguard in every company, even the twelve apostles'. So we must judge critics, not by the destructive few, but by the fair-minded majority. I like critics. I drink with some and would gladly drink with each and every one before or after a show. We are all critics but most of us do not possess the requisite courage to sign our names. Then there are those abominable scum who write anonymous letters!

One needs no qualification to be a critic no more than one needs a qualification to be a writer. There are many unforgettable witticisms attributed to the critics but since these are well-documented already I feel I would be doing a disservice to my readers were I to resurrect them.

I will turn my attention instead to amateur critics whose outpourings never find their way into the pages of newspapers and more's the pity because for unbridled savagery and merciless disparagement they are in a class by themselves. My first introduction to the amateur critic occurred in my native town. A number of us had been to a show in the local hall. The presenters were a small touring company who have long since folded. One of their group had written a short new play. He further compounded the crime, according to one local critic, by acting in it and producing it.

As we discussed the play afterwards in a local public house we invited the opinion of an amateur actor from the area who generally never had a good word to say about anybody or anything.

'This drivel,' said he, 'is an insult to our intelligence. The author should be hung, drawn and quartered. He should be hung for acting in it. He should be drawn for producing it and he should be quartered for writing it. In another country,' he concluded, 'he would be taken out and shot.'

Then there was the night I met a holidaying priest in Ballybunion. This took place a long time ago. It happened in the Central Hotel of the time, a great haunt for visiting clerics. He was seated despondently on a stool with his back turned to everybody except the barmaid.

'Finish that,' I advised, 'and have another.' He declined graciously for all his despondency. It transpired that he had not long before attended a performance of *Othello*. 'I will never be the better of it,' he said, 'and imagine I was fool enough to fork out a florin in order to sit for nearly two and three-quarter hours in suffocating conditions listening to an arrant scoundrel massacring Iago, Iago that gem of parts which has never been truly mutilated until tonight.'

I sympathised with him for I have seen bad Iagos in my time and bad everything.

'Never mind,' he said as he attracted the barmaid's attention and instructed her to proceed with the filling of two small Paddies. 'I had,' he went on, 'intended visiting a retreat house for the remainder of my holidays, a prospect which I cherish not. Fortunately I have tonight amply repaid for my occasional transgressions during my agony watching and listening to Iago. I may now with impunity defer my retreat house visit till next year and spend the remainder of my holiday in Ballybunion.'

Then there was the touring group who were dominated by one egotistical actor. They came to Listowel and they very nearly conquered. The actor in question, it transpired, was from the Irish midlands but he had a beautiful Wimbledon accent acquired we knew not where. Many praised him but there was one gentleman, an amateur actor, who loathed him. When he was accused of being jealous all he said was: 'As the candle's flame deludes the moth so does the cultivated accent delude the fool.'

Then we had a critic who used to send scathing reviews to a local paper. He was a failed amateur actor himself. He had this to say about a visiting actor who impressed everybody and went on to fame afterwards: 'He passed himself out in the first act,' he wrote, 'and never quite caught up with himself in the other two.'

Amateur critics may not make the headlines and may not be remembered but, believe me, I would be more afraid of a disgruntled amateur critic than a row of professionals.

My own first play, *Sive*, when it was first produced in Listowel received mixed reviews from the local critics but, alas, none vicious enough to recall. Maybe they are there but unfortunately the author is often the last person to hear averse criticism of his own work.

I was luckier with my second play, *Sharon's Grave*. In a pub afterwards a critic had this to say: 'Not satisfied with the great parts provided by Shakespeare, Sheridan and O'Neill, Keane put his fingers to his nose and dived deep into his psyche, surfacing after two hours covered in his own curd.'

I wrote the play while convalescing from a sore back. 'Would that he had broken his hand instead of his arse,' was the comment of the neighbour who always really meant what he said.

So you see gentle reader how kind the professional critics are by comparison! The difference is that the professional sees new plays nearly every night whereas the amateur may well have to wait a generation, during which time he becomes soured and this is reflected in his criticism. Thanks be to God for that say I.

There was another actor who used to come to Listowel on a regular basis when I was a garsún. He was nicknamed 'The Spumer' and you shall see why. Apparently when he lost his head and was carried away with a role he covered several of the rows beneath the stage with spittle and spume. They say a picture is worth a thousand words and that is probably the reason why a local publican who chanced to be in the middle of a week-long booze up arrived at the theatre one night with an open umbrella.

Then there was the critic who came one night from Tralee to see a play by Samuel Beckett. I accompanied him on the occasion and I was truly amused when the curtain came down. Not so my friend.

'What sort of review are you going to give it?' I asked.

'Nobody knows,' he said. 'You don't know. I don't know and they don't know.'

'You have me confused,' I admitted.

'Look,' he said, 'It's quite simple. If I don't understand a play I'm going to make sure that nobody else understands it either.'

Street Hazards

Now a word or two about street hazards. Your common or garden lane, boulevard, mall, arcade or ordinary, everyday street which is used solely by pedestrians is more fraught with hazards than the average battlefield. I know. I speak as a pedestrian who would rather walk ten miles than drive one in a motor car. Therefore I am aware of the hidden pitfalls.

Your average pedestrian causes little damage to his or her fellows. By ordinary pedestrians I mean those who are unencumbered by parcels, handbags, messages or grocery bags, canes, umbrellas, pots, pans and what-have-you. Those in charge of vehicular traffic, ie, prams, unmounted bicycles, shopping trolleys, roller skates, etc, have a special responsibility and should, I feel, be made undergo tests of the strictest kind in order to reduce street accidents.

Until lately I thought I had seen every possible kind of street hazard from the least harmful to the most harmful but last week I saw an instrument of destruction on a par with a tank.

I chanced to be looking out my upstairs window at the time. From this relatively safe area I have a fine view of the goings-on along the street opposite. I can recall memorable incidents from this passing parade for the edification of my readers and I can pinpoint the hazards which may lead to their downfall.

There I was watching the summer bloom on the

many females who had come downtown or into town for the day. It was a colourful and happy scene with chattering pairs and larger groups exchanging pleasantries and sometimes more scandalous titbits about friends and neighbours. Musical laughter from scandalised and amused females came faintly to my ears and I knew that all was well with the world. When women laugh out loud on our public streets there is no danger on the horizon.

Then this hellish apparition appeared. In years it numbered fifty give or take a few. It was positively of the masculine gender. It was squat, tousle-haired, unwashed, unkempt and unapproachable. It was a man with two large gallons of paint in his hands. I would reckon that each container held at least five gallons and that the man transporting them was in one hell of a hurry. I would say with certainty that he was not a painter despite the fact that he was transporting paint. Painters don't hurry. Rather do they proceed carefully and painstakingly in much the same way as they paint.

The paint transporter's first casualty was a middle-aged woman. She was struck by one of the gallons in the midriff and was put sitting on the bonnet of a nearby van, her groceries scattered far and wide. He never noticed. Next, he clashed with a man who was tying his laces on a window sill. He was knocked to the ground but he was quickly on his feet. Before he had time to remonstrate the paint transporter had disappeared around the corner where the resident corner boy had already taken evasive action. Unaware of the

149

trail of destruction in his wake the transporter kicked open the boot of an ancient car and deposited both gallons therein. Then he drove off. I had never seen him before and I hope I never see him again.

All he had to do was to bring a small boy or girl with him or a father or mother or uncle, aunt or in-law from the vast ranks of the unemployed and in the hands of any one of them place a small placard where-on might be boldly written in red letters 'Danger. Man with paint cans coming'. This would give everybody a chance to get out of his way.

Failing that he might employ somebody to walk in front of him with a handbell which might be rung loudly and continually while the paint was being transported. I felt it necessary to warn pedestrians of dangerous transporters of this type. I may be saving lives as a result.

Equally effective would be a klaxon of the type used in automobiles until recently. I would even go so far as to say that the garda síochána should be con-tacted before the transportation of the paint begins. The garda should be a uniformed member of the force. Only then should the paint transporter be allowed on to the street. The guard should accompany him all the way to his destination thereby preventing mayhem and maybe even murder.

I hope my readers will not regard me as an alarm-ist. Let me assure them that I am anything but. I am merely acting as any responsible, concerned citizen should.

If further havoc has to be averted on our streets,

precautions will have to be taken. I would be all for the appointment of a warden who would be provided with the powers to arrest would-be trouble-makers.

There is another type of pedestrian loose on our streets who needs to be removed from the scene before serious damage is done to innocent members of the general public and he is the man who reads a newspaper as he goes from one place to another. I saw one of these 'newsances' lately knocking a blind man to the ground and I am ashamed to say that the Alsatian guide dog accompanying the blind man took no corrective action.

A prison sentence should be imposed on such wretches and I am sorry to say that for a brief while, early in my career as a playwright, I too was a 'newsance'. It all began when I bought a daily paper one morning in O'Connell street so that I might read the review which the paper's drama critic had written about my latest play. It was a good review and as I was about to start reading it for a second time my progress was arrested when I bumped into a pedestrian. He was a very large pedestrian and I came off second best. He seized me by the throat.

'Why don't you look where you're going you creep,' he shouted and then as he passed on, 'suppose you bumped into a pregnant woman.'

I learned my lesson and as a result I no longer read notices while walking along streets. In fact I rarely read notices these days because I am now so old that all my works have been reviewed several times already.

Mistaken Identity

Herbert Beerholm Tree's definition of a friend is worth recalling: 'His face shining like Moses, his teeth like the Ten Commandments all broken.' It is perhaps not as good as a Dublin producer's description of a colleague who had a crick in his neck: 'He's like John the Baptist,' said he, 'with the head stuck back on by a drunk.'

No. These are not cruel descriptions. Rather are they accurate. If it is cruel itself it's being cruel to be kind for lesser or vaguer delineations can lead to all sorts of trouble as I know to my cost. When I was younger I was sent to Listowel railway station by a neighbour who had a bad leg. I was instructed to make contact with his brother who would be arriving off the six o'clock train. For the aforementioned physical reasons the neighbour was unable to go himself and since my father had informed him that I was always available for any commission however menial the neighbour filled me in regarding his brother's physiognomy, age and other characteristics.

The bother was that he had not seen the brother for years and might never see him again but for the fact that the expected visitor had lost his wife in an accident and had decided to seek consolation among his own.

'You'll see to him,' the brother cautioned, 'you'll take his bags and bring him straight here.' He thrust his hand into his trousers pocket and shook the silver coins therein. He withdrew none.

'There'll be something in it,' I was promised.

It was an easy enough task. I was to look out for a man with a long nose, bushy eyebrows, straight as a telephone pole without a rib of hair on his head. At the station I dutifully and respectfully enquired from an official if the train would be on time and he answered that it would. 'It's just after leaving Abbeyfeale,' were his exact words, 'and bar an earthquake it will be here at six.'

I have long maintained that there are few sights as exciting as a train drawing into a railway station, a train which bears kinsfolk or visitors and heaven only knows what other unexpected potentates. Surely enough the train was on time. Hissing and puffing and grinding the engine imposed its will upon goods and passenger carriages alike. Several people stepped down from the train but there was no sign of my man. Some of those who stepped down stepped back again after a few moments of exercise and one of them, a man with a mohal of black hair, after inspecting the dial of his watch, spat noisily between his rather large feet before cursing everybody within earshot including myself. I decided to look in the carriages but there was no trace of a bald-headed man with bushy eyebrows, straight as a pole, etc.

Disappointed I returned to the man who had dispatched me in the first place. He was disappointed too but tended to lay the blame on me.

'You must have missed him,' he said bluntly. He

went on to disclose that his brother was an extremely sensitive fellow and if he drew the conclusion that his arrival had been ignored it was more than likely that he reboarded the train and headed for Tralee.

'You're sure,' he said, 'that you didn't see a man taking out his dentures, looking at them and putting them back in his mouth again.'

'I saw such a man,' I said excitedly.

'And why didn't you go forward and tell him who you were and who sent you, you bloody eejit!' He shouted the words.

'Because you said nothing about false teeth!' I reminded him. The upshot of the ruction was that he had to hire Francie Malone the taximan to take him to Tralee where he was reconciled with his brother. I saw the brother that night. I had received several bum steers from the brother with the bad leg and nothing for my trouble. Firstly the man I was to meet was not bald. He wore a black wig. He was not as straight as the proverbial telephone pole. The years had played several tricks on the poor fellow. They bent him for one thing and they made him lean to one side for another. The bushy eyebrows had gone, plucked no doubt by some eyebrow plucker or other, commonly found in cities. All the brother at home had to tell me was the habit the visiting brother had of taking out his teeth to see if they were all there. Herbert Beerholm Tree would have told me.

Innocent Bystanders II

This, I promise, will positively be my last word on the subject of the innocent bystander. I know. I know. I have made promises in the past about corner boys but in those instances I was not strictly to blame for my readers persisted with accounts of the foibles of their own corner boys and one ignores one's readers at one's peril.

I hereby now swear by the shinbones of all my male ancestors and by the clavicles of all female ancestors that this is my final contribution on the thorny subject of innocent bystanders.

Not long after my first piece on the subject I was approached one night in this here bar by a middle-aged chap of rather cautious outlook. I say he was cautious because he had me under observation for a long period before he decided to tell me his story. To further prove his caution let me say that he drew me to one side lest he be overheard.

It transpired that he and his late, lamented father were in the town of Listowel one night after a horse fair. He had been no more than twenty at the time whereas the father was full fifty-five. They had over-stayed their leave having disposed of a rather cantankerous bay mare for a far better price than they had expected. As a result they celebrated until the midnight hour.

They then visited a takeaway where they purchased a sufficiency of chips and sausages.

'Now,' said the father, 'let us make tracks for our Morris Minor while we have legs under us.' So saying he went out into the street followed by his son. Unfortunately that was as far as the son got because a row had just begun nearby and he was a curious fellow, not in the least like his father.

'Hold on!' he said and he crammed his mouth full of fried sausage as he watched a bunch of prime bucks get stuck in each other.

'Come on!' the father called as he moved out of harm's way. In fact he moved the whole way to his Morris Minor where he devoured his chips and sausages in comfort.

As soon as his son had swallowed the hastily-masticated sausage he withdrew a handful of chips from the carton. Alas they were never to reach their destination for as he conveyed them from the carton to his mouth he was struck on the point of the nose by a fist.

Immediately he fell to the ground where the red blood spread from his broken proboscis. His chips were arrested in their fall by an observant urchin and a surprised canine would later enjoy the two sausages which the poor fellow had not been given time to consume.

He was assisted to a safe area by a good samaritan. Later he arrived at the Morris Minor to find his father sleeping the sleep of the just. The son explained what happened while the parent tut-tutted his sorrow. He did not upbraid the young man as he might have nor did he say I told you so.

He started the car and drove homewards but as they proceeded into the countryside he made an observation which the son quoted for me.

'If,' said the father to the son, 'you will look at my dial you will see that it has no blemish or break saving one wart which has never done me any harm and which is a danged sight better than two warts or a broken nose. The reason I have no other mark is because I saw my father get a wallop of a fist as he was watching a row at a football match. I saw the man who struck him but I bided my time for I knew the world would catch up with him and so it did for he was beaten senseless outside a dance-hall some time after.'

'What's the moral?' the son asked.

'There's no moral,' said his father, 'except that you have a broken nose and I have not.'

So we see gentle reader how foolhardy it is to play the role of innocent bystander attracted to areas of trouble. Innocent bystanders are frequently shot in the United States of America and in other less civilised states they are beaten up by police and sent to jail. These police maintain that innocent bystanders are not as innocent as they look or as they pretend to be.

Lest I forget it altogether I should perhaps recall an incident which may be of some benefit to the reader.

It so happened that it was the final night of Listowel Race week which is also the night of the All-Ireland Wren-boys' Championship. A huge crowd had gathered in the town and among them was a callow youth who began his night in these very premises. He drank his share with some other youngsters and I must say that he was more genial in drink than he was when he was sober.

The various females who served behind the counter from time to time were all agreed that here was a very charming young fellow indeed. He was curly-haired and, for some strange reason that I simply cannot fathom, it is a well-known fact that females are well-disposed towards curly-haired chaps in this day and age as they were when I was a garsún.

Anyway, as I have said, our young friend enthralled every female in the place with his lack of guile and smile and curls. He was frail and pale and self-effacing. There was something about him I couldn't quite put my finger on and then, moments after he left the bar to go down the town, it dawned on me. He was a martyr. Pure and simply that's what he was, a martyr. Others might say that he was cannon fodder.

Sure enough later on in the time he was struck a blow in the jaw for no reason whatsoever. It was my own daughter who told me the story. She had been passing by with a friend when they saw him sitting, covered with blood with his back to the wall of a house. For no reason, or so my daughter maintained as did her friend, the curly-haired boy just chanced to be watching a fight with his hands in his pockets. Need I say more. The inevitable happened which goes to prove that no innocent bystander is safe while he is bystanding.

More Interesting Titles

DURANGO
John B. Keane

Danny Binge peered into the distance and slowly spelled out the letters inscribed on the great sign in glaring red capitals:
'DURANGO', he read.
'That is our destination,' the Rector informed his friend. 'I'm well known here. These people are my friends and before the night is over they shall be your friends too.'

The friends in question are the Carabim girls: Dell, aged seventy-one and her younger sister, seventy-year-old Lily. Generous, impulsive and warm-hearted, they wine, dine and entertain able-bodied country boys free of charge – they will have nothing to do with the young men of the town or indeed any town ...

Durango is an adventure story about life in rural Ireland during the Second World War. It is a story set in an Ireland that is fast dying but John B. Keane, with his wonderful skill and humour, brings it to life, rekindling in the reader memories of a time never to be quite forgotten ...

IRISH SHORT STORIES
John B. Keane

There are more shades to John B. Keane's humour than there are colours in the rainbow. Wit, pathos, compassion, shrewdness and a glorious sense of fun and roguery are seen in this book. This fascinating exploration of the striking yet intangible Irish characteristics show us Keane's sensitivity and deep understanding of everyday life in a rural community.

LETTERS OF A MATCHMAKER

John B. Keane

The letters of a country matchmaker faithfully recorded by John B. Keane, whose knowledge of matchmaking is second to none.

In these letters is revealed the unquenchable, insatiable longing that smoulders unseen under the mute, impassive faces of our bachelor brethren.

LOVE BITES
and other Stories

John B. Keane

John B. introduces us to 'Corner Boys', 'Window Peepers', 'Human Gooseberries', 'Fortune-Tellers', 'Funeral Lovers', 'Female Corpses', 'The Girls who came with the Band' and many more fascinating characters.

THE RAM OF GOD
and other Stories

John B. Keane

The Ram of God is another collection of fascinating stories from the pen of one of Ireland's most popular writers. Who can resist Keane on 'Is Cork Sinking?', 'Fear', 'Weird but Normal', 'Proverbs', 'Illusions of Grandeur', 'English Words but the Accent is Irish' and many more intriguing topics – a must for all Keane fans.